L. P. HOWARTH

SWARF

Catnip

CATNIP BOOKS
Published by Catnip Publishing Ltd.
14 Greville Street
London EC1N 8SB

This edition first published 2010
1 3 5 7 9 10 8 6 4 2

Cover design by Nick Stearn
Cover illustration by Teresa Murfin

A CIP catalogue record for this book is available from the British Library.

ISBN 978-1-84647-103-2

Printed in Poland

www.catnippublishing.co.uk

Contents

1. The Seeding

Ant spotted the cat across the garden. 'Midgeley, you idiot, come in!'

The sky was darker than it should've been for that time in the evening, the rain was thick and – *green*. No doubt about it. Actual green rain. Weird. Ant darted across the garden. His hands found the Midge on the compost bin. As he flung the tabby over his shoulder, a pillar of darkness stepped out from behind the telegraph post in the corner of the garden. Electricity lines crackled overhead as green dust settled over them and the current flashed across.

Ant couldn't move a muscle. His body tingled with fear. He couldn't cry out, he couldn't move so much as a little toe as a dark figure stepped out from the shadows. A second figure joined it. Ant saw that they had faces, and he fell down onto the grass, and the figures approached him, and there wasn't a thing he could do about it. White-suited legs moved around him, conversing in a series of clicks, a metre from his own safe, bright living room, blazing behind drawn curtains.

A shifting face, close to his. Ant screwed up his eyes tight.

Something's happening. It's important young seeds understand. The voice hissed inside his mind.

'Who are you?' The cat's heart beat against Ant's chest. 'Why me?'

This seed has red hair. Long fingers stroked his face. *Seeds with red hair are like meteors, and do great things. This one, this one will do.*

A tap on his forehead and Ant felt information streaming into his mind in a collection of flashing images, faster, wider, more wild, until he felt as though his brain would burst.

Another tap on his forehead, and Anthony Granville Hatt sat up and wondered what he was doing flat on his back by the flowerbed, with green dust settling over his chest. He'd come out for something – the stupid cat. Midgeley's eyes shone in the darkness and green dust settled in ridges along his whiskers; and around the corner of the house, the bonnet of the car glimmered green under the single village streetlight.

The wind gusted through the trees and Ant got up and thought he might've been talking to the telegraph post in the corner of the garden. A clicking like busy insects grew fainter in the darkness – something released him – and at last he could scoop up the cat, and go inside.

He didn't say a thing to anyone. There were only vague whispers in his mind. Anthony Hatt watched telly as usual till ten, then went to bed as he always did, and he slept as unconcernedly as if he'd never been interviewed by strange beings in his garden; and he dreamed, that night, that the world stopped turning and that cars fell off it in streams. Slower and slower it turned, until the oceans fell off as well.

In the morning, everything was silent. Ant went downstairs. The front door stood open onto the garden, and his father's car wouldn't start.

'What's wrong with it?'

'No petrol.'

'Then get some.'

'Something's happened to petrol, all right?'

Something's happening. It's important that young seeds understand. Ant shook the echo out of his mind. 'What? What's happened to it?'

'If I knew that, I'd be halfway to work, wouldn't I?' His father looked annoyed. Ant went in and flicked on the telly. *No one's* car would start, not in Exeter, Bristol, London – Paris or New York. Green dust had fallen over the entire world. Overnight, petrol had been transformed into a strange green gel and everywhere engines were locked solid. Ant returned to the front door.

'It's that stuff!' he shouted. 'They're calling it Swarf – like Swarfega!'

He actually went into the garage and dug out a pot of the green jelly hand-cleaner. Its black-and-white label read *SWARFEGA Hand Cleaner for Most Mechanical Engineering Jobs*. He took it outside to the car. The green jelly bleeding out from under the petrol cap looked exactly like it.

'Don't touch it,' warned his father, dipping his hands into the *SWARFEGA* and wiping them with a rag.

Ant poked the 'Swarf' with a stick. The car wasn't out of petrol. It was just that *petrol had changed.*

2. Swarfed

That had been two days ago – two days of panic and warnings about electricity rationing. Swarfed petrol tankers lay on motorways like giant sausages. Nothing could be delivered to power stations, or anywhere else. Ant wandered into the kitchen at ten past ten and turned off the telly. Most transport was dead, diesel was as solid as petrol – and there was hell up in Tarmouth, the city on the horizon where the river met the sea – so what was new?

The local newspaper lay on the table. It would be the last Monday edition of the *Westcountry Herald*. Strange omens had been reported from far and wide. A cook at the Satellite Café had suffered a burn in the shape of an alien face. A local company had volunteered a hot air balloon to take her to hospital. She'd enjoyed the journey as much as anything in her life, the paper reported. She was backing the appeal for propane for the emergency medical balloon's burners. A picture showed her holding a notice: PLEASE HELP.

Ant wandered next door. Now his parents were packing.

'Keep an eye on Nan, can't you?' Jen, his mother, straightened.

'Where're you going?'

'Help on Uncle Connor's farm – all the machinery's Swarfed.'

'But –'

'Nan says you can stay with her, till things get back to normal.'

Ant looked at his father. 'We'll be back soon,' Frank promised. 'I've been laid off at work, anyway.'

'And stay away from the quarry where that lad drowned,' his mother shouted after him, half-an-hour later, as he set off for Nan's on his bike with a rucksack the size of a child.

Toiling up to the Top Road, Ant passed stranded cars in the strangest places. Someone had abandoned a Vectra in the children's playground outside the Punch Bowl Inn. All four doors hung open, and a scarf trailed out onto the slide. A Swarfed Tesco Home Delivery lorry had veered into the Chapel car park, and waited there for its bags of fresh groceries to go mouldy.

Neil Griffiths, Ant's neighbour, had his bonnet up outside his girlfriend's house. 'Swarfed solid,' he told a handful of gel, in disgust. 'What *is* this stuff?'

'Petrol,' Ant slowed. 'Haven't you heard the news?'

'Been working nights, haven't I?'

'My Mum's left your Mum a note. Can you feed our cat, I'm going to Nan's?'

'How'm I supposed to get there?'

'Walk? Hitch a ride?'

'Who from?'

The empty main road looked back at Ant.

''Orrible old gluey green stuff – where's it come from?'

'Green rain, the other night?'

Neil looked at it. 'When's it going?'

Ant cycled on. At last he came out onto the Top Road running along the ridge. The road was as deserted as a football ground after the stands had emptied, but terrific gouts of steam shot into the air beyond the opposite hedge. He stopped by a *GIVE WAY* sign, though there was no one to give way to, and waited for Fred Salter's traction engine, a huge clanking thing like a fairground ride, to chuff out onto the tarmac. Fred Salter was a neighbour of Ant's grandmother. Though his workshops were two fields away from her cottage, complaining about Fred Salter gave Nan something to live for.

The traction engine bore down on Ant with a rumble that still took the bottom out of his stomach, though he was used to it by now. He was used to the ear-splitting hissing of its various valves, used to the spinning of its dangerous-looking flywheel, the clank of its steering chain, the thunder of its wheels, the rattle of its scarlet canopy bearing the legend *Kitty Hamley*. It looked like a humongous Thomas the Tank Engine with a roof and solid rubber 'tyres' on its enormous wheels. It ran on coal and water, and chuffed out steam. Fred had explained the pressures that drove its pistons, but Ant had to ask again, every time Fred gave him a ride.

At last Fred was near enough to hear him. Ant waved. 'Where're you going?'

'Brewsters!'

'The pasty factory – why?'

'Spuds!' Fred slowed by pulling back on the reversing lever and jerked his thumb towards the tender, or wagon, behind the engine. 'Got a load of Pentland Dell from Landover Farm!'

'Potatoes? But they can't send out pasties.'

'Limited production only, they rang me yesterday.

Me and the old lady –' Fred meant the *Kitty Hamley*, '– we're the only thing on wheels for miles.'

Now Ant could make out the stamp which said *Best Pentland Dell Potatoes* on the sacks destined for the factory down the road, where his father worked. 'You must have three tonnes up.'

'Four.'

'They've cut back,' said Ant. 'They told Dad not to come in – now he and Mum've gone away.'

'Where're you off to, Nan's?' Fred pushed back his cap. 'Hop on, if you want a lift.'

Ant hopped on and lifted his bike into the wagon so it bobbed along on top of the spuds. From his perch in the cab of the engine, he looked back at it now and again. Then he forgot all about it in the joy of 'coaling' the engine with heaping spadefuls when Fred threw open the blazing firebox, and steering a bit, when he didn't. He almost, but not quite, forgot what was always at the back of his mind as they rumbled over a stain in the road that, not so long ago, had been a badger. Stu Diamond had rescued badgers. When Stu Diamond had been alive.

Ant took down his bike at Cudlipps Corner and watched Fred steam away until the chuffs of steam disappeared over the hill towards Cabbytown, or

'Carburyton', as the road signs would call it. He turned his wheels uphill, and at last the pokey little cottage under the crossroads showed him its crooked chimney.

His grandmother was taking biscuits out the oven, as she so often was if they happened to call by on a Saturday morning. But today everything was different. Ant chucked a chicken out of an armchair and flopped down beside the Rayburn.

'Come to stay with you.'

'What's that, dear?'

'I'm staying a few days, till this stuff's gone.'

'What stuff is that?'

'Green stuff, gungeing up engines – you know.'

Nan poked a cake with a knitting needle. She eased the cake back into the oven and closed the door. 'Where's Mum and Dad to?'

'You mean, where've they gone?' Ant disliked the way Nan lapsed into Cornish. 'Over to Connor's farm,' he said, lapsing himself. 'Connor dun't know what do, with no tractor.'

'Tractor's broken down?'

'Fuel tank's solid with Swarf – haven't you been watching the news?' Ant helped himself to a biscuit from a cooling rack on the table. Either the raisins were extra chewy, or the biscuits were all wrong today. He took something out of his mouth – a piece of meat. Ant stuck it tactfully behind a teacup. She'd been making pasties, as well, and had got mixed up, somehow. Also Nan's eyesight was going.

Now she seemed to be stuck looking into the oven: 'What about Dad's work?'

'Brewsters is on half-time – no lorries going out.' Ant bit into a bun. 'Still making pasties for locals, though. Fred Salter's delivering spuds.'

Nan wobbled and made a grab for the sideboard and a plate spun off it into the dog's basket. Her old terrier, Billy, raised his head.

'Nan!' Ant jumped up and steered her into the armchair.

'I'll be alright...directly.'

Ant fetched her a drink. His grandmother fanned her face with a tea towel the colour of mud. Come to think of it – Ant looked around – everything in the little kitchen was the colour of mud. Nan should move to a care home. Maybe his mother was right.

She sat clasping and unclasping her hands. 'Cars've stopped, you say.'

'Everything's stopped, 'cept Fred.'

'Don't talk to me about Fred,' Nan said, fretfully. The yellow clock on the wall made a little jump with the extra-loud tick it gave, occasionally. Billy stretched and got up, standing on three legs and scratching as he got out of his basket. 'How'll the ambulances run?'

'They won't.'

'And they've stopped because of green stuff...in the engines.'

'After that green rain.'

'And the doctor, he can't come.' She worried the subject like a dog with a shoe. 'How'd Mum and Dad get over Connor's?'

'Cycled. He was meeting them halfway, with a hay cart.'

'So nothin' on wheels, you say?'

'No.'

'Things goin' wrong all the time,' Nan grumbled, unfolding a grey handkerchief and folding it again. 'Worryin', if you got a murmur.'

Nan was convinced that her heart skipped a beat now and then. It was a Topic of hers. The timer dinged on the cooker. Ant took the grisly tea towel and gingerly fished out a cake spotted with what looked like cherries.

'Like some cake? He'll cool off in a minute, or two.' Things were always 'he' in Nan's dialect. 'Chocolate sponge in the pantry, if you don't...fancy fruit.'

She seemed a little breathless and confused. Ant

remembered the meat in his biscuit. 'I'm good – can I go upstairs?'

'Go where you want to, lovey. I'll just rest me eyes a...bit.'

Leaving her snoozing in the armchair, Ant crept upstairs. The pullout bed he'd slept on as a child still grated out from under the spare bed, if you forced it to. He pushed it back again, remembering the wallpaper and the early-evening light glancing off it, when he'd been put to bed at seven while the adults laughed downstairs.

At least now he'd have the room to himself and go to bed when he wanted. He unpacked his rucksack and opened the window. The road to the stone quarry, and the smooth green lake which had filled up the diggings, stretched away over the heath. Once again he felt the urge to see into its depths, be alone with the wind which moaned round it. It moaned about Stu Diamond. He had to let it wrap itself around him sometimes.

He slipped downstairs like a ghost. Nan was still asleep. Letting himself out of the back door, he scrambled the bike up and over the spoil heaps of some forgotten mine, or other. Then setting his wheels into the well-remembered ruts, he took the long track up to the quarry.

3. Quarry Lake

He'd seen him around, of course, before he'd got to know him, but that was it. No one spoke to Stu Diamond, much – he was too weird, plus he hung out on Quarry Hill watching birds and animals, and was hardly ever in school. Ant'd first properly crossed paths with him on this very road leading up to the quarry. Nature Boy had been dead for a couple of months now, but he haunted Ant's thoughts like a barn owl, swooping in and out of the darkness at the back of his mind.

The lake was grey today, and a fire burned on the little beach. There were six of them, two in wetsuits. Mark Biggins sat on a rock with a Red Bull. 'Cool that this Swarf stuff's hanging around.'

'Because?'

'No school buses, dummy.'

Ant regarded him coldly. 'Thought we agreed not to come here.'

'*You* do.'

'Not tombstoning – why would you do that?'

'To remember him?' a quiet voice answered. 'It's two months today, to the day.' Kim Diamond, Stu Diamond's cousin, offered Ant a can. They were toasting *him* in Red Bull. Ant nursed the can between his palms as, one by one, the crew remembered things they had to do, and slipped away.

Mark peeled off his wetsuit on the other side of the little beach. Kim glanced at Ant: 'You were the one who saw him last.'

'Who says?'

'Mark.'

Ant cracked open his can and felt the Bull sear his throat.

'You spoke to him last, right?' Kim persisted.

Ant crumpled the can.

'What did he say?'

'Nothing much.'

'How did he look?'

'Not great.'

'So why –'

'Fit in, how do I know?'

'Is that what he said – to *fit in*?'

Ant watched the crew parting where the track left the heath. Nature Boy had been a one-off. He would never, in a gazillion years, have been one of them. He was too extraordinary.

'You were up there, you could've stopped him.' Kim pointed to a pinnacle named The Point, looming dark against the sky. Beneath it the cliffs swept down to the silent lake. 'How could he even *think* –'

'I told him not to jump.'

'He always was such a dufus.'

Ant shrugged. His throat was too full to speak.

'They said he was drunk – was he?' Kim waited.

Drunk with anger, maybe. Ant remembered the outrage in Nature Boy's eyes, the day he, Ant, had first found him rolling a run-over badger out of the road with his foot. Ant'd stood over it, too. *Something's going to happen, to stop this*, the boy in the anorak had told him. *Yes*, Ant'd said, meeting his eyes. *Going up on the hill?* He'd felt drawn to Stu by his intensity. He was like someone many decades older than himself, yet also like someone born yesterday, who didn't understand why bad stuff had to happen. Only later had he, Ant, learned that the Geek on the Hill was Stu Diamond, the boy who was never in school. 'No way was he drunk, that day.'

'What, then – depressed?'

Ant shrugged again.

'You hung out with him,' Mark accused, coming

over, packing his wetsuit like a dead man into his rucksack.

'We never hung out. We just did stuff like bird watching now and again . . .'

'More'n you did with me.' Mark pulled Kim to her feet. 'See ya, wouldn't wanna *be* ya,' he told Ant.

'Smell ya, didn't wanna tell ya.'

Mark didn't laugh. He turned coldly away. Hard to believe they'd been best mates. Ant watched as he walked away, hand-in-hand with Kim.

Long after the crew had melted away over the hill and the afternoon had begun to fade, Anthony Granville Hatt sat by Quarry Lake. The remains of a mouldy buzzard's nest wagged in the wind under the Point, and a chilly breeze curled over the water and shivered it against the rocks. The fire had gone out long ago and only a few charcoal remains smoked on the little beach. The second time he'd met Nature Boy had been on this very spot – he'd wandered into the quarry on his way to Nan's, and had spotted him on the beach. 'Yo.'

'Keep it down, can't you?' Stu Diamond had flapped his hand. Your classic bird-watching anorak, Ant'd thought. Right down to the hat and the gloves – who wore gloves, if they weren't six, or sixty?

He'd squatted beside him, anyway. 'What are we watching?'

'Fledgling buzzards.'

'Where?'

'Not very observant, are you?'

'Don't sit up here all day watching birds like a big freak, do I?'

Stu Diamond had handed Ant his 'snocs, which was what he called his binoculars, and Ant had scanned the fluted granite walls under the Point – there!

'Chicks look like Muppets – see 'em?'

Heads and necks in an untidy nest – Ant nodded, thrilled. What he'd said had been a bit harsh. *Don't sit up here all day watching birds like a big freak, do I?* But he had a mouth on him, as his father said sometimes.

Now stern walls of granite looked down on Ant and judged him, and ripples chased one another over the lake as if there were fishes in it who might have had something to say. Its depths glinted with old fridges and car-wrecks – car wrecks which two months ago, a slim lad had 'tombstoned' into, for the first and last time in his life. Orange tape still wagged over the water from the Accident Investigation. Ant and Mark had steered clear, said nothing, no one but the granite walls had known they'd been there, that day. Now Mark had split to Kim. The wind moaned. Ant hugged his knees.

This was why he came back. Nature Boy had lingered so long in the green world of rubbish down there at the bottom of the lake that he'd had to be dragged out, and some part of him remained there, still. Ant hunkered into a crevice and stayed there until he was thoroughly cold. He deserved to feel cold. He deserved a lot of things. He came back here to punish himself – to remember not to forget the burden he carried.

Presently he dozed off and dreamed that Stu Diamond held a bloody badger in his arms and told him *They'll pay*. And he dreamed he replied *I know*, and Nature Boy's knife chimed against the side of a car . . .

Clink-clink. Clink.

Ant opened his eyes and remembered he was in the quarry. A party of climbers moved over the opposite wall. It was the clinking of their equipment which had awoken him. Cracks crossed the fluted granite sweeping down from a dizzying height. Along one of them, something red moved.

'Mind that!' someone shouted. *That – that!* echoed the quarry.

Ant shrank into his crevice. Now that he could focus, he made out Mark Biggins's dad, a Sergeant with the Territorials, his harness flashing red on the rocks. Sergeant Biggins was big and scary, and always away on Exercises, or grim over his paper when he wasn't. Ant tried to make out what the men strung below the Sergeant, like the charms on a bracelet, were up to. They seemed to be stowing something in, or retrieving something from, a deep cleft in the rock, Ant couldn't quite see what. Then the sunset flashed off something metallic – a canister of some sort. The charms on the chain passed another canister, and another – and a linking chain seemed to pass them out of the quarry.

Ant craned forward.

A truck waited, just in sight, at the side of the entrance. He leaned forward a little more, and a stone rolled off the little beach and plumped into the lake with a pop like a cork coming out a bottle.

'Hold hard, there!' *Hard, there!* the command rattled round. Ant leaned into the shadows as the Sergeant's gaze swept the beach. 'Who's there?' *There? There?* quizzed the quarry walls.

No one, Ant tried to telegraph back.

'This is Restricted Access – whoever you are, go home!' *Home!* The walls rang, sternly. Ant's heart hammered.

'I'm waiting.' *Waiting – waiting.*

Now all the climbers had turned.

Ant came out of his crevice like a greyhound out of a starting trap, and bolted away on the path. A man and a horse, both wearing masks over their mouths, stared at him from around the side of the truck. Ant ran past his bike, past the crossroads in the track, past the turning to Nan's, past mine-heaps, past the cinder-slope beneath them, past Nan's compost bin at the end of the garden, past her chicken-run, and past the chickens. He didn't stop till he reached Nan's half-hatch door, and bolted it behind him.

'Nan?' No answer.

He opened the firebox door of the cooking range. It reminded him of the firebox door to *Kitty Hamley*. The fire was low, the nuts of fuel burned out. He shook in fresh black nuts from the coal scuttle and the fire blazed up nicely. Nan had taught him the ways of the Rayburn a long time ago. Solid fuel ranges are like people, they need constant attention, she'd told him. You can't just walk away.

'Bill, come on, then – what's up?' Billy, the old terrier, stood trembling in the corner, where the door made a dark triangle with the wall behind the settee. 'Stupid dog – want some supper?' Ant found a crusty can of dog food in the corpse-cold pantry and scraped some out for Billy. He opened Tupperware containers and made up a plate of food for himself.

Then he set it down and went upstairs and listened outside Nan's bedroom door, and pushed it open a little: 'Nan?'

She'd gone to bed early, after her 'turn'. Nine was her bedtime, anyway. He went downstairs and ate ravenously in front of the Rayburn – cold sausages, half a pasty, scones, and a wedge of fruit cake the size of a book.

Then the phone rang.

'Dad.'

'Get to Nan's all right?'

'Fine, but I've –' *been up the quarry?* '– got indigestion,' Ant finished.

'Serve you right, if you eat Nan's bread hot out of the oven – how is she?'

'Gone to bed. Make it to Connor's, all right?'

'We ditched the bikes,' Ant's father said. 'Your mother's chain broke and I ran into some idiot in front of me, so we walked to Painter's Cross and Connor met us in a hay cart. You're all right at Nan's, aren't you? We'll be back before you know it.'

'How?'

'Mum sends love – she's still milking. Generator's Swarfed, it's a nightmare. Take care of yourself.'

Dad, I'm scared. 'And you,' Ant managed.

'It's only a petrol hiccup – temporary hiatus, the

Prime Minister says. Might be out of phone contact for a while, reception's intermittent.'

'Dad –'

'Mum says to look after Nan and keep clear of that quarry. Speak again soon. Bye.'

Ant replaced the phone. 'That you wheezing, Billy? Got a cold?' He patted the terrier's basket. 'Come on, then. Good old dog.' Billy barked twice, sharply. He wagged his tail and sneezed and put down his head on the floor at the side of the settee.

'Stay there, then.' Ant put up his feet and watched telly, restlessly switching channels to avoid the news. Still bulletins announcing Breaking News ran along the bottom of the screen. Nothing seemed to have changed. In fact, things seemed to have got worse. The lights went out at midnight as the Emergency Power Curfew came into force. Ant threw open the firebox door, and only the glow from the Rayburn lit the dim living room. The scene at the quarry replayed itself in his mind. Had the Terries been stashing something, or taking something away? Secret supplies of petrol – how else could they run a truck? It must've – *had* to have been – their emergency supplies underground. And not Swarfed? How?

The dog wheezed softly in his corner.

'Shut up,' Ant told him, sternly. 'Time for bed.'

4. Spence

Next morning, Nan's house was silent except for the chickens outside. Ant supposed someone should feed them. He necked a bowl of old-lady cereal in the kitchen and wondered what to do about the Rayburn. He should get some coal. Nan should be up. The world should be tackling Swarf.

'Billy, are you *still* there?'

Despite being invited upstairs, the old terrier had slept behind the settee. Ant tipped some dog biscuits onto the floor in front of him. He made Nan a cup of tea and arranged some toast on a plate. At least there was power this morning. He found a tray, even made it nice with some primroses. He climbed the stairs and knocked, then breezed in.

'*You* went to bed early, last –'

His grandmother wasn't in bed. No one was. What he'd thought had been Nan's form in the dim light last night, had been an old-fashioned bolster. Ant looked all round the room. He stood in the tiny bathroom with his tray, wondering where she could have gone.

Billy barked sharply downstairs. The bark went to Ant's heart. He took the stairs three at a time, vaulted the settee and tore back the living-room door to reveal a pair of slippered feet.

'Nan! Oh, no – not *all night!*'

And she must've been there all the time he was guzzling sausages in front of the telly, ignoring the wheezing in the corner, like an idiot. Now she moaned and turned over.

'An...thon...y.' Her breath came in gasps.

Billy barked and jumped round her, as if to show him how hard he'd tried to communicate. Ant brushed him off.

'How long've you been out of breath like this?'

'Day or...two. I...dunno...'

Ant remembered she'd collapsed – had it only been yesterday? Now he felt desperate he hadn't picked up on the situation earlier. 'You never said.'

'Lungs is filling...up. Doctor give me...diuretic.'

'What's that?'

'Makes you...go. You know.'

'When did the doctor call?'

'Friday.'

She couldn't've been this bad. He searched for something to say.

'I'll...beat it...yet.' His grandmother lay back, exhausted.

Hospital, now, Ant decided. He got up and fetched a glass of water and held it to her lips. At least the room had been warm. He fetched a blanket and covered her.

'I'm here, now,' he said. 'I 'spect you were coming to find me, when you –' *fell behind the door and lay undiscovered for hours.* He couldn't believe what he'd done. 'I'm going to get help – can you stay here a sec?'

She found his hand and squeezed it. 'Can't do... nothin' else...can I?'

'Back in no time, all right?' He went out in a businesslike way, as though the doctor were waiting outside. A blaze of sunlight blinded him. Ant stood blinking on the doorstep with the wide world spread at his feet to the shining horizon, and not a functioning ambulance in it. *Nan,* he thought. *Oh, Nan.* For a moment he felt like panicking. *Come on,* he thought. *You can fix this.* The morning had warmed into the beginnings of a nice day. Sunlight flooded the neighbouring fields. He began to walk down the hill.

*   *   *

'Health Centre – hello?' No signal, yet again. Ant scanned the fields for someone – anyone – to help. He crossed a pasture, then another. A gleam of chestnut showed through the next hedge. This was the meadow bordering the Top Road, where Spencer, the chestnut gelding, mooned over his gate and occasionally accepted tidbits from Ant.

'Here, Spence, what have I got?' Spencer cocked his ears. Ant could tell he was following him on the other side of the hedge. After a moment, the horse appeared at the gate.

'Here, then! Spence!' Ant showed him a Tic Tac. Spencer stretched out his neck. The grey tongue manoeuvred the tiny treat between his tombstone teeth. His eyes rolled up while he crunched it.

'You'll have to walk for another.' Ant opened the gate. The lane bordering Fred's land stretched away up the hill. Suddenly Ant saw that he could lead Spence to Fred Salter's workshops, huddled beyond the next hedge. A horse, and something to pull Nan in – that was a plan. Though it would mean borrowing – stealing – Spence from owner, or owners, unknown. Ant left a note. *Back soon*.

Inside the *Kitty Hamley*'s shed, the air was still moist from the morning's getting-up-steam, but the engine itself had departed. An old boiler that Fred was re-riveting took pride of place in front of a curtain at the end of the workshop. Under the ceiling ran the belts of a contraption powering various lathes and grinders. Over the walls hung sinister-looking scythes, horse brasses and strange bits of harness. Tack, Ant thought it was called. He picked up a heavy leather collar, and replaced it on its hook with an effort. What was he doing here?

Spencer began to munch something from a bin labelled 'Mangolds' – they looked like whiskery swedes. One of them rolled under the curtain at the back of the workshop and stopped against something with a thump. Ant walked over and threw back the curtain. The outlines of a scarlet cart stood out as his eyes got used the gloom.

Red was Fred's signature colour, all right. Ant walked all round it one way, and all round it another. Large wheels at the back, smaller wheels in front; a smart driver's seat, with a whip; a flat bed that someone could lie on, full length. The tailgate folded down to make steps – ideal. But time was ticking away. A lick of excitement flickered up in his chest, as Ant wondered if he could do it. Spencer, plus a cart, equalled transport.

First he should catch his horse.

He took down a rope from the wall and got it over Spencer's head while he was busy crunching mangolds. He felt proud of himself for getting this far. Now what? He took out his stupid mobile and tried the doctor again. This time he got through: 'Health Centre? It's an emergency. Three, Underhill Cottages –'

'No callouts, I'm afraid – we're Swarfed.'

Of course. 'But –'

'There's a waiting list for Emergency transport.'

'I've got a horse and cart, I –'

'Better head for Crebberton Hospital.'

'What about Tarmouth General?'

'Crebberton,' the voice said. 'Good luck.'

Ant stared at his phone. Tarmouth was bigger, with a Heart Unit – why shouldn't Nan have the best? It would be up to him to get her there; it was up to nobody else.

'Good old Spence. Come on, then.' He led the horse to the cart and tied him to one of the shafts. At least horse and cart were together. Spence nibbled the plush of the driver's seat. 'Stop that,' Ant told him. The impossibility of harnessing the horse *between* the shafts and going anywhere soon, made him hopeless. He hoped Nan had stayed where she was, on the floor. Another fall would top things off nicely. Nan, the hospital – a horse, and a cart. The jigsaw spun round in his brain. No one was going to do it for him – he would have to force the pieces together.

Fred's dingy 'office' area caught his eye. He took out the Yellow Pages and scanned it. Finally he dialled a few numbers on the grubby landline: 'Brimblecombe Riding Stables?'

'Hello.'

'D'you know how to harness a horse to a cart?'

'A cart?'

'Four wheels,' said Ant. 'You know.'

But Brimblecombe didn't know. The next stables didn't, either – or the next. Finally Ant picked out riding schools at random: 'I've got a horse and cart. I don't know how to harness them together.'

'Jingo, is it?' a gruff voice asked.

'A what?'

'Type of cart. Postie'd come by in the jingo, when I was a lad – jump up, he'd say, and give us a lift. Seventy years ago, that was.'

'It's got big wheels and small wheels, and she can lie down in the back,' Ant gabbled. 'Please can you tell me quickly, I've got to get her to hospital?'

'Got a horse, you say?'

'Spencer.'

'Is he there, then?'

'Yes.'

'Right then, you'll back him between the shafts. You'll find a collar to go over his head. You'll find a bit, with blinkers attached –'

'Wait.' Ant took the phone to the wall and lifted down the heavy collar. One by one, the right bits and pieces wanted him to lift them down and lay them out on the bench. One by one, the voice over the phone told him how they went together – stuck with him, while he was bribing Spence between the shafts with mints and working out how to attach him. 'He look all right?'

'He looks fine.' Ant walked round Spencer. The collar was attached to the traces, and the traces were correctly threaded through, and correctly attached to the cart. The girth was done up; the bit, and the blinkers, adjusted. There was even a strap called a martingale, which would stop Spencer from panicking and throwing back his head. Ant had pretended to put that on – why shouldn't Spence throw back his head? 'Do I take the reins, now?' he asked.

'Is he calm?'

'So far.'

'If he isn't trained to pull a cart, he might be frightened to start with – remember to let him have his head and, with luck, he'll settle down quickly.'

31

'Thanks a million.'

'Go steady, won't you?' the eighty-year-old voice wished him luck.

'No nonsense, now.' He jammed back both doors with old tyres, climbed into the driver's seat – it was a long way down to Spencer's back – and chucked the reins once, twice: 'Gee up!'

Nothing happened. 'Don't let me down, Spence.'

He jumped down and led Spence out of the shed. Not being in the driver's seat was a risk, but he climbed back up again, quickly. Spence took a few steps, and stopped. Ant got down again and threw up an armful of mangolds into the cart.

'Giddyup,' he told Spence, smashing a mangold and buzzing a piece into the lane, two or three metres ahead. Spencer moved forward to get it, and Ant saw that greed would overcome his fear of the cart.

Throwing down tidbits in front of him every now and then, Ant brought the horse, and the cart, into the lane, and slowly coaxed them on.

5. Poor Mister Balrog

On a hillside somewhere in England, a chestnut horse drawing a red cart neared a pokey cottage. The horse had been harnessed a little too close to the cart, and his blinkers were wonky, but he stopped politely, when requested to. A red-haired boy jumped down from the cart, tied the horse to a washing line, and ran in at the open door.

The horse began to nibble an apron hanging out to dry. The wheels of the cart lodged in the stone flags and prevented him from reaching some stockings. The horse threw his head up and down and tore the apron off the line. A terrier rushed out and scrabbled beneath his legs, barking fit to burst. The horse shied in terror, but a hand claimed the reins just in time. The red-haired boy scooped up the dog and pulled down the steps, and an old woman in slippers climbed shakily into the cart with the aid of an umbrella.

The boy went back in and brought yellow and green cushions and a blanket and arranged them around her. He brought a rucksack and a flask and put them beside the driver's seat. Finally he climbed up and chucked the reins. 'Come on, Spence.'

'He's had me...apron.'

'Spence!' The horse put down its head, but the wheels were lodged in the flags. The boy got out and pushed the cart with all his might, and the horse pulled by accident at the same time. The boy jumped up again, clicked his tongue, and the red cart and the chestnut horse moved slowly out of the gate, and up the short slope to the Top Road. Once out on the breezy ridge, the boy on the cart could see for miles. Away on his right sparkled the city on the distant shoreline. To his left, reared Quarry Hill. Ahead of him the road followed the ridge until it fell away and lost itself in the plunge to the river, and the bridge, quite a way beyond which lay the little town of Crebberton.

'All right, Nan?' Ant glanced round. Her chest was working hard under her thin cardie. Mangolds rolled around her and her poor head juddered on its cushion. He felt for her, with each bump in the road: 'Nan – all right?'

'Thank...you, dear.'

Billy the dog climbed up in front and took the wind in his teeth. Luckily, Spence couldn't smell him. Ant began to feel in control – almost in control.

'Look at Sharpe's!' He pointed in astonishment.

Sharpe's Filling Station and Stores at the top of the hill was almost unrecognizable. ALL DELIVERIES SWARFED, a notice read. NO PETROL – NO DIESEL – NO GAS. The petrol pumps leaned away from one another in surprise. The Swarfed storage tanks under them had exploded the forecourt as though a volcano had sprouted overnight. A little cog shifted in Ant's brain. Whatever had sent Swarf, it *had meant to stop cars moving*.

Swarf stood in all the cracks radiating towards the Stores. A tooth of concrete had shattered the window and no one had boarded it up. Shoppers were arguing at the door. Someone broke away with a trolley filled with bread and milk, and raced away down the hill. This was where his mother normally worked. Ant had tried to reach her at the farm. He would ring her from the hospital. Just as soon as they reached it.

Now the hill was beginning to take them. Brimming with mist like a river of clouds, the valley opened on Ant's right. Out of the mist loomed the strange sight of a single-carriage diesel train marooned on the viaduct.

Nan began to slide down the cart, as the cart began to slide down onto Spencer. Ant felt panic gripping him, yet they'd barely begun to gather speed. Sand Hill was notorious. Lorries had careered down it. Floods had deluged the village at the bottom of it. Brakes had failed on it, and cars had plunged into shop-fronts.

Ant tried to see ahead. Glimpses of the road dropping away beneath them bobbed between Spencer's ears. Odd 'vehicles' dodged in front of them, propelled by people who had dressed in a hurry – supermarket trolleys, wheelbarrows, bikes laden with pets and baskets. There seemed to be a rush for the bridge.

'What's going on?' Ant shouted across to a tandem.

'Registering in town!' the tandem shouted back.

'Registering? What for?'

The tandem wove away in the crowd. The sand-filled Escape Lane rushed by him – last chance to get off the hill. Ant pulled on the reins. 'Woah, Spence, slow down!'

The long drop wound down through a village. Perhaps he could slow down there. Ant looked around for a brake and found a wooden lever. The blocks smoked as they hit the wheels, and now the cart was pressing on Spence, the shafts riding up and dragging him on, and still the hill grew steeper. Every now and then a back hoof struck his seat like a rocket. Ant felt really frightened. The cart was running away with them, and there *wasn't a thing he could do.*

'Stop!'

'How?'

'Lash them wheels...together!' Nan croaked. ''Course, they used to 'ave...drags.'

'Drags?'

'Metal shoes...on the wheels, stop 'em runnin'... downhill...'

Ant spotted a sloping driveway. He stood up and hauled on the reins. With an enormous effort he switched Spence up it, and the cart stopped dead with a thump. Ant fell out and chocked stones behind the wheels. *This is it*, he thought. *If we go on, we'll crash and die.*

Nan waved a lead in his face. 'Use this...if you... want.'

'What am I supposed to do?'

Carters had used to tie their wheels together on steep hills. She hadn't...dreamed it. She...could remember it. Nan pointed out how he could do it and Ant got the idea. It took less than a few minutes to lash the cartwheels on each side together with Billy's 'endless' nylon leash, longer to cut it with the kitchen knife Ant had pocketed on his way out. He imagined skidding downhill. He supposed it would be all right.

Turning the cart would be awkward without rolling back, but he would have to do it. 'Spence, turn!'

Ant pulled on the right-hand rein, Spence threw his weight into his collar, and awkwardly the cart came around. Ant watched out for a gap in the crazy traffic: '*Now,* Spence, you can do it!'

Now they were skidding fast into the carnival going downhill. A goldfish in a tank passed them on a donkey cart. A mother cycled by with a pushchair attachment behind her bike, and a laptop wedged beside her child. The cartwheels smoked on the tarmac. Gradually the cart slid faster, and Spencer was running for his life. Something had gone wrong –

'More...weight!'

Too late – Sand Hill had them in its grip. 'Runaway cart!' Ant yelled.

Now the wheels were screaming like rabbits caught in a trap. A man with a pram piled high with electrical goods saved himself in a hedge. Now they were skidding sideways. Ant gave Spencer his head – they straightened! A green cart barrelled by, and a donkey went down in front of it, and the cart spun on, with bloody wheels.

Ant stood up as they flashed through some traffic lights. They shrieked past a rusty post office – now his wheels were throwing sparks: 'Run, Spence, run!'

Run on, or get run down! Now he could see the river – the bottom of the hill, with a sharp right-hand turn onto the bridge, or a dive over its parapet into the water. A cyclist sped past them, somersaulting into a trailer. Ant aimed for a gap, but he struck the trailer a glancing blow, and a white hand attached itself to the opposite side of the cart.

It hauled up a hat and some sunglasses: 'You'll give Mister Balrog a lift? Yes, you will. Plenty of room!' He had a leg over the side, now. 'Poor Mister Balrog, you'll give a blind man a lift to town!'

Billy set up a barrage of barking.

'None of that,' the white face snarled, drawing up a chest, then an arm.

'Get him off!' Ant screamed, as the cart veered.

Billy snapped at him. Balrog swore. He tore off his blind man's glasses – he could see! Nan took out her umbrella and beat Balrog over the head. Balrog defended his face and eyes. He tried to snatch the umbrella, lost his grip, fell away like a rag in the wind.

Now the turn was upon them!

'The bridge!' Ant yelled. 'Hold on!' He hauled on the reins, but the sight of the river checked Spence and he made the turn with seconds to spare, and the cart jack-knifed after him and slid to a halt on the bridge. Only Balrog's black hat sailed on over the parapet and crowned the green water slipping under the arches to the sea.

Ant took out his knife and hacked his way through the mangled nylon leash fused between the cartwheels. He reclaimed his driver's seat and brought Spence tidily to the back of a queue. The bridge was black with jumbled traffic. On the opposite bank, the empty Tarmouth Road sprang away up a hill into woodland. Ant stood up impatiently – what could be going on? The voice of Balrog, bothering people behind him, rose over the murmur of the crowd: 'Poor Mister Balrog. All human beings, aren't we? You'll give a blind man a lift?'

Ant inched Spencer forward to prevent him eating someone's aspidistra. As they reached the head of the bridge, Sergeant Biggins stepped out. 'Name?'

'Spencer the horse.'

'Don't make a joke with me, sonny.'

'Ant – Anthony Hatt.' For some reason, his best mate's dad was in charge of a roadblock.

Sergeant Biggins looked up. 'Destination?'

'Tarmouth Hospital.'

'Tarmouth road's closed, due to an accident. While you're here, laddie, about the other day – at the quarry.'

'When you were moving your secret stash of petrol around, you mean?' Desperation made Ant reckless. He didn't care what he said.

'You might've thought we had petrol – in fact, we were hauling by horse. Just so you know, mass of old diesel down a mine – remembered by HQ.' He took Ant into his confidence with a friendly arm round his shoulder. 'A mile down and *still Swarfed* – just like the rest of it. Tested it all the same at Doomhilly – supposed to be Swarf-proof canisters they brought it up in, too –'

'I don't care what you're doing at Doomhilly,' Ant shrugged him off, naming the secret testing station over the hill. 'I've got to get through, my Nan's really ill –'

'Holding area. Now.' Sergeant Biggins ordered a man with a wheelbarrow to a queue behind the Old Toll House. The head of this queue was being funnelled in front of a sign saying ROAD CLOSED UNDER EMERGENCY REGULATIONS, and sent back over the bridge. He frowned at Ant. 'Is it an emergency?'

'Her chest hurts – she can't breathe.'

The Sergeant took a stroll round the cart. 'All right, Missus?' He came back around, and took Ant aside: 'Probably progressive heart failure, my old man went the same way –'

'Her lungs're filling up, she's drowning.'

'I should go home, if I were you. There's not a lot they can do.'

A four-by-four in military drab shot past.

'You could take her –'

'Electric vehicle, on limited charge, before you ask.'

'They could help her in hospital – make her comfortable on her last day on earth, that isn't much to ask, is it?' Ant sobbed. 'You could let us through, if you wanted.'

'Go home and get Registered, that's my advice,' said the Sergeant, heartlessly, 'and get this horse out of the way.'

He pushed Spencer's nose while he was talking. Spencer pushed him back with interest, and the Sergeant staggered into his second-in-command. Ant let the horse have his head, and suddenly they were barging through the roadblock, and up onto the Tarmouth Road.

'Stop where you are!' the order rapped after them.

Spence charged a red-and-white barrier, sending it end-over-end down the wooded slope under the road. They rounded a bend on a gaggle of soldiers tinkering with stranded vehicles. Someone shouted: 'Stop!'

Without missing a beat, Ant switched Spence along a track. Under overhanging rhododendrons they drove blindly into deep shade. The river rushed by, a heartbeat away. Mossy ruts guided them on. Ant recognised it, now. This was the Queen's Drive – Queen Victoria's, that was. Carriages had used to clip along it to some stately home upriver.

Soon the shouts had faded and the hubbub of the roadblock had been replaced by the deep hush of conifer plantations. No one could off-road it after them. No one could search with a 'chopper, or pursue them with a wailing police car with lemon-and-lime stripes along its side. As they whipped along the cool Queen's Drive with the river rushing beside them, Ant knew they were through.

6. The Incline

They were through as far as the tree, at least. The enormous fallen beech was the end of the road – or the end of the Queen's Drive, anyway. Ant brought the cart to a halt with a sinking heart.

The massive trunk blocked the track completely. There would be no leading the cart around it. There would be no squeezing under it, or getting Nan over it. No way could he could lead Nan on, on Spencer's back, even if she could sit there. Ant glanced back. His grandmother was sleeping, her fine hair spun over her living room cushions like spiders' webs.

He climbed down and ate some crisps. How could he ever have dreamt he could get her to Tarmouth Hospital? The river slipped on, green and glassy, in a mesmerising sort of way. Spence began to graze. Ant finished his crisps and wondered whether to let her lie here. There were worse places to slip away.

He remembered the dead hawk he and Nature Boy had found lying in the grass one day. 'What is it?' he'd asked, pushing the speckled chest with his foot. 'Poisoned buzzard,' Stu had said, bitterly. 'Now the fledglings'll die, as well.'

'Couldn't we save them?'

Stu had pointed to the nest on a giddy ledge under the Point. Some things you couldn't save, like the rabbit they'd spotted on another occasion, swimming round and round in the lake. 'What's wrong with it?' Ant'd asked.

'It's myxie,' Stu answered. 'Diseased.'

'Shouldn't we help it?'

'No.'

They'd watched the trailing ears, the straining eyes, the last struggle. The lake had closed over it, once, twice, and everything had been still

'Sorry about calling you a big freak, that time,' Ant'd got off his chest, at last.

Nature Boy had shrugged. 'I don't fit in. Like that rabbit.'

'Only 'cos you're never around –'

'I like animals better'n people. I have these dreams. These feelings. Like something's going to happen.' Stu Diamond had taken off his hat. *He* had red hair, too.

'Anthony,' Nan's voice cut through his thoughts, 'you going to fetch...your old Nan a...drink?'

Ant jumped up, gladly. 'I didn't think – hang on.'

She watched him shrewdly over the cup. 'Got through worse than this...in the war.'

'This isn't like the war.'

'Isn't...it?' Her chest worked like a steam train. Nan was fighting, all right. 'Aren't we going...on?'

'Soon as we find a boat.'

She looked up at him trustingly and Ant saw that she thought he meant it. He screwed back the cap on the flask. He knew he should 'water' the horse. It would mean taking him out of the shafts, and maybe not getting him between them again, but the going was ruined, anyway. Ant fiddled with the collar, and somehow Spence came unhitched, and he led the horse to the river trailing his traces, and watched him bury his nose in and drink.

Ant began lifting things off him. 'Might as well go free, Spence, you're no good without the cart.' Swapping sides to undo his bridle, Ant glanced upriver. Incredibly, a short distance away, a boat bobbed beside a small jetty. It was easiest thing in the world to wade up and un-loop the rope from the post where it was loosely secured; easier still, to bring it back, though normally it would be –

'Stealing?' asked a man walking a dog.

'Emergency requisition,' said Ant, taking his cue from Sergeant Biggins.

'Off to find a doctor?' The man nodded at Nan.

'Hospital,' said Ant. 'Tarmouth.'

'You're clearly a resourceful young man, but it's thirty miles.'

'Not down the river.'

'Salmon weir, a couple of miles down. Crebberton Hospital's your best bet. If you can get up the hill.'

'They tried to stop us on the bridge,' Ant said. 'Something to do with being Registered.'

'Oh, they'd like us all to be numbers, now.' The stranger laughed shortly. 'They'd like us to stay where we are, and do what we're told.'

'They have to do stuff because of Swarf. Maybe it'll go away again. It's weather conditions, or something.'

'That, or a third agency. It may have unearthly origins.'

'Like crop circles or something?'

'Why not?'

'What, aliens stop all our cars and invade us?'

'Or save us.' The stranger's eyes met Ant's. 'Want a hand lifting her in?'

'What about Spence?'

'He'll be fine.'

'Can you take him to Meadowbank, up Top Road?'

'Leave it to me,' the stranger said. 'Let's put her in the boat.'

Once Nan was settled with her cushions and Billy stood quivering in the prow, Ant pushed off with the oars, and the current gripped the little boat and bowled it along with the river. 'Won't be long, now,' he said, more cheerfully than he felt.

As a bend hid the woods from view he searched the shoreline for the stranger, but there was no sign of any figure. Ant kept his eyes on the scarlet cart until it disappeared. Anything to blank out the last glimpse of a chestnut horse grazing the riverbank, lonely under the pines.

The river carried them on at a stately pace, and Ant found he didn't have to row. Silt-lined banks slipped past them. Herons started up, and ducks were surprised about their business, as Ant and Nan swept by.

Soon the tug of the river changed. 'How far's the weir?' Ant shouted.

'Coming...up...' Nan's finger trembled as she pointed ahead.

The current began to pull them in earnest towards the weir, where a glassy shelf of water broke itself over the rocks. Ant fought to turn the boat. Billy dashed up and down, yapping. Ant dug in his left oar – deeper! Again!

He knelt up, the boat rocked, and in that moment they almost turned over – but now they were coming around. Ant's arms were on fire, but he pulled the boat into the bank, and the keel was grounding at last on a pebbly shore. He jumped out onto a drab little beach and pulled up the bow, exhausted.

He handed Nan the water bottle. 'I'm going to see what I can find. Won't be long, all right?'

Ant followed Billy up stone steps grey with slime. Around him lay the tiled wharves of Old Quay Living Museum. He remembered they'd tiled the wharves so that none of the copper ore would be wasted – heaps of raw copper from the mine, waiting to be smelted and shipped all over the world. Amazing how much he remembered from a school trip, ages ago. Now Old Quay lived on its past, and the only treasure coming out of its copper mine were damp and grumpy tourists.

Today the car parks were empty. A Swarfed four-by-four stood at Reception, but the Ticket Office was closed. A few pigs snuffled behind the Mine Captain's cottage, and between the deserted buildings a tremendous waterwheel clattered.

Ant spotted a ramp. He returned to the little beach and handed Nan out of the boat. With incredible slowness he helped her up the ramp and found her a bench on the quay. 'Stay here with Billy – I'm going to find something to eat.'

He wandered back to the waterwheel and watched it clatter round, reminding him of the day of the school trip, when they'd all been dressed up as miners. In the nearby forge hung the costumes the tour-guides wore – a blacksmith's leather apron, a mine captain's bowler, dusty black dresses worn by 'mine maidens'. He crossed the village square and stepped through a broken window into the Gift Shoppe. Someone had been here before him and had rifled the boxes of fudge. Stocking up on biscuits, he headed back to Nan. 'Gingerbread Men or Cornish Fairings?'

'Where'd you...buy 'em?'

'I didn't. Someone else got the fudge.' Ant ate five fingers of Heritage Shortbread washed down with Devon Spring Water and considered the situation. They'd crossed the river and travelled along it, but looming in front of them between Nan and Crebberton Hospital towered lofty Morden Down.

A bonnet blew by trailing lace and ribbons, slap onto the side of the waterwheel. Ant watched it carried twelve metres into the air as the wheel filled and emptied its buckets, and the weight of the water pushed it round. This wheel was just for show. But on the hillside above them, another giant wheel turned.

'What's that waterwheel in the trees for?'

He wandered over and read the Information Board: *Water Power In Action*, said the board. *An Incline Railway brings copper from the Friendship Mine.*

The black tunnel mouth of the Friendship Canal yawned at the top of the inclined, or sloping, 'railway'. Rusty orange wagons shuttled *up and down it*. The sides of them were low. You could practically step in, and take a ride up the back of Morden Down.

Ant walked smartly back to Nan. 'Come on – they go up the hill, and they're empty.'

'What's...that...dear...?'

They crossed the square painfully slowly and Ant showed Nan the wagons shunting around the turn. Suddenly Billy jumped into one.

'Is it a...ride?'

'It is, now.' Ant pulled Nan in after him, and they were shuttling away up the slope. In minutes the Museum looked like Toytown. Far beneath them snaked the river. Ant pointed – there was their boat, still filled with living-room cushions, lemon, gold and green! Beyond its distant meanders, the river shone away to the sea as the lovely valley Ant called his home gradually revealed itself. A buzzard wheeled high in a blue sky – he knew what a buzzard looked like, thanks to Nature Boy. He hoped Stu's spirit was free. Again that burden of guilt.

Ant looked ahead, anxiously. A passing place prevented him from seeing what happened at the top of the incline – and now they were rattling higher, and pine-dotted slopes rushed under them; now they were lurching round the banana-shaped passing track, and being dumped off it, again.

'Oh!' Nan said. 'My life!'

Now the dark mouth of a tower loomed at the top of the incline. Ant could hear the wagons complaining as they were shuttled around the turn. He tried to picture the mechanism – gearing powered by the waterwheel bucketing round. The rails gleamed, the wheels clanked, vibrations ran down the chain hauling them closer. Pine needles rushed beneath them – they were coming in to meet the slope! With a jolt, the winding drum took up the slack. The chain was bringing them in – its jaws opened in front of them – closer – closer – into the very mouth of the tower!

Another lurch, and Ant fell forward and took Nan with him, and Billy sailed over their heads. Then they were rolling in pine needles, and the sky and the leaves and the ground were all mixed up in a tumble across bumps and hollows until at last the leaves settled, and everything was calm.

7. Flowers at Heartsease Cross

'Nan?' Ant sat up and knew he'd killed her. His grandmother lay cold and still. He'd pushed her off an incline railway – and only a short scramble away from help. Incredibly, the edge of the Crebberton Road topped the leafy slope through the trees – for all the good it was now. Now the dash downhill had been wasted; the struggle to escape the weir, the trip uphill in the rusty wagon – everything had been wasted. Missed the boat, again, hadn't he? He'd failed to get Nan to hospital in time. Being late was his speciality – that, and putting his foot in it, something he got from his mother, his father said. He'd failed to save Stu. Now it was happening again –

'It's those...big 'uns, you got to...watch.'

Ant spun round. His grandmother's eyes were

open and she was talking at the sky. 'When I was a little girl, I thought you could...bump into 'em.'

'Clouds?' Ant lay back, his heart pounding. 'Nan, are you all right?'

'Father's pal took us up in a...small plane. I couldn't've been more'n four, screamed...blue murder, I did – Mind the clouds, we'll crash! Father says, hush! We'll fly...through 'em – watch! And off we tilts, into the..mist. No! We'll crash! Screamed and screamed, I did. Father says, well, better go down...ruined the flight, I did.'

Ant tried to picture her as a little girl. 'What colour hair did you have?'

'Scraggy old...brown stuff...like the back end of a chicken, mother said.'

He pictured her on the common. It hadn't been so long ago, that they'd used to go there together. 'Remember when we went blackberrying, and you fell in that bush? "Don't make me laugh, it hurts," you said.'

Nan felt in her pocket and passed something over.

'Nan –'

'You got it coming. Have it...now.'

She handed him something, and he opened his hand. Ant held up the magical crystal umbrella handle he'd wanted since the age of three, and the light winked through it in shades of amethyst, brown and blood-wine. He'd always, always wanted it. *You can have it*, she'd promised him at three, when fairytales had loomed large on her knee. One day, she'd said. When I'm gone. She'd been hooking blackberries towards her with the crystal handle when it had still been attached to an umbrella, the day she fell into the bush.

'You just toppled over,' Ant remembered. 'Just stuck on top of the bush – took me ages to pull you off.'

Nan closed her eyes. 'Don't make me laugh, it... hurts,' she said again, like she used to.

Heartsease Cross said the road sign. Ant squinted across the empty crossroads and picked out the flowers on the wall at the gloomy junction. They'd rejoined the Crebberton Road at a notorious accident black spot.

'All clear.' He'd let Nan rest under a bush near the edge of the tarmac. 'Come on – think you can make it?'

It had once been a place to take a breather on the long pull uphill. Now a nasty junction with the main road had led to a steady stream of accidents – the last, a motorcyclist, over a year ago, now. Faithfully since then the flowers marking the scene of his death had been renewed every two or three days, as though not to let cars forget.

Cars were murderers, thought Ant. They got away

with it every day, and breezed around as though nothing had happened. Most motorists sped past the spot, ignoring the cushion of violets or carnations on the wall – Ant himself had sped past. Now the ghosts of the place moved around him. He could picture the motorcyclist's mother, creeping up through the trees. *What you got there, Ma? Carnations?* the motorcyclist would ask, crossing his legs on the wall. Ant shivered and set a foot on the tarmac, and turned to hand Nan up.

'Where d'you think *you're* going?' a rough voice called up the road.

Ant dropped back down the slope. 'Keep still, someone's coming.'

'Poor Mister Balrog,' a familiar voice whined. 'He just needs a lift up the hill.'

'How did you get across the bridge?' Sergeant Biggins appeared in the middle of the road. He must have been watching the crossroads. He signalled, and a sentry snapped up. 'Escort this gentleman back down the hill to the Holding Area.'

Balrog protested. 'Need to get Registered in Crebberton, don't I?'

'Got family there, have you?'

'Wouldn't ask, if I hadn't.'

Ant risked a second peek. The Sergeant examined

Balrog coldly. 'Seen a boy in a red cart? Grandmother on board, black-and-white dog –'

'Saw – met 'em on Sand Hill. I'm blind see? That's why I need to get through –'

'Where are they now?'

'What's it worth?'

Nan made a grab for Billy, but her fingers fumbled and Billy shot out onto the road. Darting straight for Balrog, he circled him barking with rage.

'You again, damn your hide!'

'You need to tell us anything you know,' Biggins continued. 'Withholding information can be an Offence under Emergency –'

'I tell you, this is the dog!' Balrog whipped off his dark glasses. 'They're somewhere – over there!'

'Privates Green and Prisham, escort this gentleman back to the bridge.'

Balrog swore.

'No need for that. When you're ready.'

Before he knew what was happening, Balrog was led away, protesting that he had a bad leg and couldn't walk very far.

'Corporal,' said Biggins. 'Search that slope.'

Ant put his finger to his lips and closed Nan's eyes with his hand. He scattered leaves over her like remembrances. *Pray they don't have dogs.* As an afterthought, he took a toffee out of his pocket and threw it a little way away. Then he pulled close his own covering of beech leaves. *Pray they don't use Bill to sniff us out.*

But of course, they were going to: and in moments, the search had begun.

'Good dog – where are they, then?'

Ant found Nan's hand under the leaves. This was too much for anyone. Billy snuffled close. Closer.

'All up?' someone asked.

'Thought he had something,' a soldier's voice sang. 'Looks like it's only a sweet!'

Gradually the soldiers moved away towards the river, and as the sounds of them beating bushes with a stick grew fainter, Ant thanked his lucky stars that as a search dog under Emergency Regulations, Billy was as good as a bath sponge. It was just Ant and Nan now. They'd taken Billy with them, his last bark died on the wind.

When at last the silence of Heartsease Cross had settled over them once again, Ant brushed himself off and found Nan. 'The road's too dangerous,' he explained, 'but we *could* slide back down to the waterwheel and go along the Friendship Canal –'

Nan panted. 'Listen.'

The clop of horse's hooves echoed more loudly up

the lane to the junction with every passing minute.

'I've just *given* you the last mint,' a voice was complaining. 'You can't want another *already*.'

Ant jumped up. 'Watch out, your old man's about!'

'I know.' A red cart stood at the crossroads, a familiar chestnut horse sweating between its shafts.

'What are you *doing* here?'

'Clamp it and hop in, Hatt.' Mark Biggins reined in Spence. 'You want a lift, or what?'

'How come you're rescuing us?' Ant asked, as they jogged along again. He regretted leaving Nan's lemon and lime cushions – they would probably have gone over the weir.

Mark shrugged. 'Any reason why I shouldn't?'

Plenty. Ant struggled to remember the last time he and Markie had hung out together without the Stu Diamond thing getting between them. 'Are we ever glad to see you –'

'Saw you go off on the Queen's Drive, all right? And I don't much like what my dad does,' Mark went on, 'turning people back all the time – she going to be all right?'

'Not unless I can get her to Crebberton.'

'Be there in under an hour.'

'You reckon?'

'That's her best chance, isn't it?' Spence toiled around a long bend, with Mark urging him on with the whip.

'You don't need to do that,' said Ant.

'How'd you get your Nan up the hill?'

'Incline railway.'

'No way.'

'How'd you find the cart?' Ant countered.

'Easy. Down by the river. Man helped me harness him up.'

'What man?'

'Some bloke walking his dog. He said he thought you'd get off the river at Old Quay and come out at Heartsease Cross.'

How could the stranger know? Ant struggled to remember him. For some reason, his face was a blank.

'Dad was watching the hill, so then Spence 'n' I came up the shortcut,' Mark finished. 'How's she looking, now?'

Ant climbed into the back of the cart and wedged Nan against the side with a blanket. It felt good to have Markie on board. Sunlight shone pink through Biggins's sticking-out ears. Ant thought of saying, 'Good to have you on board', but decided it was corny, the kind of thing Nature Boy would say. Instead he stopped Nan's head from rolling from side to side and wondered what the hospital might have in the way of food. An explosion from Spencer's backside interrupted his thoughts.

'Farts a lot, doesn't he?' said Mark.

Ant climbed up to join him again.

'Think they'll work out how to get rid of Swarf?' Mark asked.

Ant considered. 'No.'

'Dad says things could get serious. What d'you think's going to happen?'

'Nothing. It'll be all right.'

'How d'you know?'

Ant saw that Mark was frightened. He struggled to catch a fleeting thought by its tail: 'I dunno, I just do.'

They jogged along together and something of the old connection, before Stu Diamond had come between them, seemed to lie in the way Mark handed the reins to Ant, and he, Ant, chucked Spence on, round the corner. But the rhythm of his hooves changed and Spence began to toss his head. Finally he stopped.

Ant looked down. 'What . . . ?'

Pasties in the road! They dotted the white line and lay in mounds under the hedges. Spence picked his way between them. It was as they were rounding the bend that they came upon the abandoned lorry with its nose in the hedge. BREWSTERS WHEN YOU'RE PECKISH, announced the usual flash along its side, like a wall blocking the road ahead.

Mark whistled. 'No way.'

A cascade of meat pies had spilled over both carriageways. Premium Steak pasties lay everywhere, like some random giant's tantrum had flung them far and wide. Ant jumped down and peered into the back of the lorry: 'Not much left in here.'

'Stinks, does it?'

'Not really.'

'When did it happen?'

'Duh – when everything got Swarfed?' Ant read a batch code on a Luxury Steak & Mushroom. 'Correction. These were only made a couple of days ago – why aren't they dated the day before the green rain?'

'What?'

'The truck. It would've set out really early.'

Mark frowned. 'You lost me.'

'Why aren't the pasties rotting by now, if the truck's been here since Tuesday? And why aren't they clearing them up?'

'Have to leave the scene of an accident undisturbed, or something?' Mark guessed.

'How long's the road been closed?'

'I don't know – why?'

'And anyway, it's the wrong route – London orders go up the motorway.' Ant was certain, now. 'There's no way you'd find Premium Steaks on a minor road like this.'

Mark looked at him. 'What d'you mean?'

'They staged an "accident" to stop people passing this place.'

'Why? What place?'

Ant rescued a hat labelled *Brewsters Bakery* from its carefully arranged place on the white line. He put it on and the cold sensation around his head seemed to clear his brain.

Morden Down loomed ahead. Funny that an accident had blocked the road at the nearest point to Doomhilly. Funny that it was at the secret testing station on Morden Down, where Swarf was being investigated.

'Doomhilly Testing Station, of course.'

8. Dead Zone

'Patrol, up ahead!' Mark scrambled down from his perch on the cart. 'What d'you want to do?'

Ant had been thinking for two whole minutes. The gloves were off, he realised. They didn't want people going this way. Now there was nothing else for it: 'Go cross country, what else?' Taking Spencer's bridle, he led him towards the hedge.

'What are you doing?'

'Getting past this lorry, before they reach us?'

'But –'

'Help me guide him, will you?'

It was an impossibly narrow gap. Nan moaned as the cart hit the side of the hedge. Spence shied a little at his reflection in the giant wing-mirror as Ant led him past the cab, but he put down his head and pulled. 'Good boy.' Ant led him on, and now the cart was jammed in the gap.

Mark ducked, too late. 'They're coming down the road!'

Helter-skelter, he tugged the horse up the ramp, and into the back of the lorry; Ant pushed Spencer back. Thinking on his feet he minimised noise by steering them onto the cardboard which was scattered everywhere. He dashed back and hooked closed the doors, as the first of the soldiers appeared.

'Nan – all right?' Where was she? Ant felt along the back of the cart, but it seemed to be filled with soil. A giant shelf of turf had peeled off the hedge and covered her. Silently, desperately, he began to claw out giant tussocks.

'Stop where you are!' a voice bellowed outside.

A score of marching boots all stamped together.

Ant found Nan and held her hand. 'It's all right, I'm here,' he whispered.

'You, you and you, guard the road,' the voice outside went on. 'A fugitive named Hatt is in the area – boy with red hair, driving a cart – may have an old woman with him. We've been asked to bring him in. Company B, come with me.'

'You take the hill – we'll stake out the lorry,' another voice said, after most of the feet had clumped away.

'Thanks for nothing, Dawkins.' One of the sentries marched off.

The cab shook as someone dropped into it. From the sound of it, they were rifling the glove box. After a while they grew bored and began swapping jokes in the road.

'Skeleton goes into a bar, says "Give me a beer." Bartender says, "Anything else with that?" "Yeah, I'll have a mop."'

The lorry boomed as one of the soldiers banged the side of it. Spence tossed his head.

'Good boy,' Ant whispered.

'So what's with this Hatt boy – thieving?'

'Some kind of top-level thing. Alert's on for redheads, they say.'

'Oh, yeah?'

'Yeah, they're casting *Gingas from Space*.'

At last the sentries moved away to brew up some tea on the bend. Ant broke open a pasty for Spence, and watched him nose cold potato. Nan was as bad as could be, and as cold as the clods that had covered her. Ant fingered the crystal umbrella handle in his pocket. It symbolised better times – cosy times together. Half buried in the back of a cart – this was her lowest point yet. He squinted through the cab. The sight of the soldiers brewing tea on the corner made him feel desperate.

'I've got to get her out of here and get her something hot to drink.'

'Satellite Café's round the corner.'

'What about Forrest Gump outside?'

'They'll go back to base, when it's dark,' Mark hoped. He nodded at Nan. 'She asleep?'

Ant took her hand and she stirred. 'Are we there ...yet?'

'Having a rest, for a bit,' Ant hushed her.

Nan nodded and closed her eyes again. Her arms felt colder than ever. Trapped in a lorry, not knowing what would happen next – Ant wondered if this was how calves felt. He'd often seen the bewildered eyes and crammed bodies while stuck behind cattle transporters in traffic. You only had to be stuck behind a cattle truck once to take a long, hard look at the next meat pie you ate.

In the silence Spencer shifted his legs and dropped a huge raspberry which rattled around the lorry like a hundred whoopee cushions going off at once.

'That's blown it.'

'Literally.' Mark made a face.

Spencer farted again, even louder.

'What was that?' a voice called.

Ant held his breath. He sneaked a look. The sentry called Dawkins was crossing the road.

The others had put down their cups. Moments later, light flooded in as Dawkins threw open the doors.

It was hard to hide a horse and cart in full view. Ant got up. He went a little way towards him down the ramp, and tapped Dawkins smartly on the forehead.

'Anything?' one of his mates called.

'The wind,' said Dawkins, accurately. It was as if he'd never seen them. He turned and let the doors swing shut. 'Fancy a hand or two?'

Ant heard him walk round the lorry and climb up. The other soldiers joined him in the cab and they began playing Texas Hold 'Em poker.

'How did you *do* that?' Mark whispered.

'I don't know.' Images flashed across Ant's mind, as though something had woken them up. 'Someone did it to *me*, and *I* forgot. In the garden. After the green rain.'

'Forgot, what?'

'Dunno, I can't remember.' *Red seeds are like meteors – this one, this one will do.* Yes. He'd been tapped on the forehead. The words echoed deep in Ant's brain. In the cab of the lorry the poker cards came and went, and bets were made and lost. The Flop, the Turn and the River, the dealer's hand was called – once they'd shown their faces, players decided whether to bluff or to fold.

He thought about his own turns of fate, his bluff that he could drive a cart, the river that he'd crossed somehow. Spencer had weed like a fountain, and the smell of it filled his nose and his throat. Ant sighed and held Nan close. It was going to be a long afternoon.

Ant sank his teeth into a doughnut and the jam oozed out and filled his mouth. He was about to move on to a plate of chips, when Mark Biggins woke him up. His heart sank. They were still in the lorry.

'Halt!' cried a big voice outside.

Clump-clump! A score of boots stood to attention.

'We're moving out and taking over the old radio station for the next couple of days,' the officer shouted. 'Any sighting of the Hatt boy, hit the big red emergency button outside. Dawkins – anything to report?'

'Clean bill of health, Sir.'

'In English.'

'Nothing to report. Sir.'

'Very good, we'll call it a day. Company B – when you're ready!'

Ant applied his eye to the door as the Company marched past in smart order, Dawkins struggling to pack up his billycan as he went. The faces filed by – kind faces, stern faces, flushed, dismal, craggy faces – Balrog! The pale figure faltered along, his black coat clapping behind him in the wind. 'Don't push a poor, blind fellow – have a heart.' Ant watched, actually sorry for Balrog, as his escort marched smartly behind him.

As soon as the road stood silent, 'Open the doors,' Ant ordered. He reclaimed Spencer's bridle, and Mark put his shoulder to the cart: 'Back, Spence! You can do it!'

Nan moaned as the cartwheels jolted off the ramp. Ant looked at her anxiously. He shook out her blanket and tucked her in. 'Satellite Café's round the corner. Can you hold on till then?'

'Can't do...much else...can I?'

It was her old joke, but made with less spirit this time. Ant wished he could take up the cart and throw it over the hill to the hospital. Instead, he took up the reins and urged Spence on. Soon the Satellite Café was coming into view round the corner, with its dumb 'Organic Food' sign swinging in the wind.

'Hello? Anyone?' Mark and Ant wandered in.

The funky wooden counters stood empty, and the muffin basket hadn't a crumb in it. *Hedgerow Surprise,* announced the Specials Board. *Rose-Hip Pancake with Yoghurt.* Even that sounded good. Ant parted a bead curtain. In moments he'd searched the fridge.

'Anything?' Mark joined him.

'If you like carrots.' Ant found a carton of iffy milk and tipped it into a pan. He clicked the ignition button on the cooker a million times. 'Out of gas, as well.'

There wasn't even Cuppa Soup in this house of lentils and beans. Finally he boiled a kettle and made hot Marmite for Nan.

Mark scanned racks of gummy-looking bottles. He was raiding the cupboards for cereal, when he noticed the finger holding a door closed. 'You can come out, now,' he told it. 'We're looking for soup for his Nan.'

The finger thought for a moment, before the cook stepped out with a pan: 'You never know who'll come in, next – nettle and lentil all right?'

'Didn't think anyone was here.'

'They tried to move us out, but we hid.' The cook lifted a curtain hiding rubbish bins, and a tiny girl crept out. 'This is Alice, she collects berries.'

Alice put her finger in her mouth. The cook heated nettle-and-lentil soup, and Alice looked into the café: 'There's an old lady, outside.'

The cook smiled. 'Bring her in.'

'Are you the one with the burn?' Ant asked. 'I saw you in the paper.'

The cook peeled up her sleeve. 'They said it looked like a face, I don't know why, I'm sure.'

It was a funny burn, Ant thought. He'd seen a vague face like that before, but then – 'Read anything into it, couldn't you?'

The cook laughed. 'These are strange times – people see omens in everything. I'll say one thing for 'em, it's a nice ride to the Burns Unit in the Emergency Balloon.' Her quick hands flickered between pans in the homely café kitchen, all hung about with garlic and old-fashioned herbs. 'Pity they're out of propane – they can't get fuel for the burners for love nor money, now.'

'I'm taking my Nan to hospital.' The thought of the unfriendly outdoors made Ant wish he could shrink into the inglenook, or stay behind the bins with Alice.

'Quick run over the hill,' the cook agreed. 'Stay out of *their* way, mind – Doomhilly, I mean – this enough for your Nan?'

She doled out bright green soup and Ant took some to Nan, who brightened at the sight of a cup, as much as she was able; and Alice timidly brought out scones, and took out carrots to Spence. Then the cook found baked potatoes as big as Alice's feet in the back of the oven, and Mark fried himself an egg and felt as if he was human.

It was a long time before they felt like going. But the struggle for breath was becoming terrible. Nan was using up her last ounce of strength, Ant could see. 'Time to move on,' he announced.

Alice waved goodbye from the top of the hill.

Suddenly Ant turned back. Fetching something out of his pocket, he pressed it into her hand. 'Here,' he said. 'It's magic.'

Alice held it up, and the late afternoon sun lanced through it in shades of amethyst, brown and blood-wine. She was still looking through the umbrella handle when Spence turned up towards Doomhilly – there was no avoiding it – and Ant knew he'd given away the talisman that would be his when Nan died.

That was because she wasn't going to. He hadn't saved Stu.

He *had* to believe he could save Nan – if *he* didn't, who would?

For three-hundred-and-sixty-five degrees around the secret testing station, nothing moved or crawled. In the dead zone around Doomhilly, Swarfed tractors stood silently in fields and no one tried to fix them or bring in the sheep, and pubs called The White Hart and the Ring O' Bells lay empty with hooded beer pumps, and the shops and businesses were still.

'Main gates ahead,' Mark warned. He knew about these things from his father.

Ant stood up to see Doomhilly. He'd never seen beyond the perimeter fence. Now he glimpsed a range of low, white buildings on a windswept airfield. The neat fields ran up to the fence. Behind the fence stretched a jungle of grasses and wild flowers.

'They'll see us,' Mark warned.

Ant urged Spence into a wide dog-leg around some gorse bushes. His plan had been to follow the fence, and cut across the fields to Crebberton. Now an open stretch of moorland yawned before they could get off the road.

'Head for the North Installation,' Mark said. 'That way, we're not far from the hospital.'

'You want to drive?'

'You're all right.'

Ant felt panicky and annoyed. He could practically see Crebberton over the hill – if only he could blast Doomhilly out of the way with a death-ray or something. Now the range of low buildings which made up the Chemical and Biological Testing Station looked disappointingly ordinary. Some people called it a spy station, there'd been such a fuss about the unearthly-looking radar dishes snooping on transatlantic emails. There were always rumblings in the paper about ancient 'nerve-gas' dumps leaking into some old canal. Yet butterflies flashed in the grasses of the perimeter zone. *Conservation Site,* a sign boasted. *Our unsprayed meadows are home to a wide variety of wildlife.*

Ant took the cart in a loop around some ponies. Spence snickered to them as he passed. They were rocking over a puddle, when an amplified voice announced: 'YOU. OVER THERE.'

Ant froze, but Spencer clopped on.

'STEP - AWAY - FROM - THE - CART!' the huge command blared over the heath.

Ant glimpsed a mounted soldier with a megaphone.

'Why'd you bring us this way, you idiot?' he hissed at Mark.

'Yeah,' Mark said. 'I'm an idiot – like your mate Stu Diamond'd know better.'

'Leave Stu out of this.'

'*You're* the one who brings him back in!' Mark took the whip and cut Spencer with it. Ant tore the whip off him. Spencer began to rear.

'I got to...go, dear,' Nan moaned. 'Please don't let him...jolt...us...'

Ant fought to regain control. Mark fought to stay on the cart. Nan moaned and held her bladder.

'Get off, you're tipping us up!'

'You!'

A dozen annoyances burst in his brain like a zit, and he felt all the grief and confusion he'd suppressed for so long, spilling out of it. He hardly knew what he was doing. With Mark's elbow in his face, Ant fought his best friend in plain view of the military patrol riding out to pick them up.

9. Red Seed

'Some best mate – you *always* liked Stu better'n me!' Mark couldn't let it go.

'Got Kim, haven't you?' Ant retorted.

'She dumped me. If you'd told her what happened – it wasn't *my* fault either –'

'Shut up!' Ant screamed. 'Shut up, shut up!'

'That's all, lads!' A soldier mounted the cart and tore them apart. Ant felt so angry, he could've killed him. Next moment his anger had melted and he felt embarrassed for Markie, standing sniffling and wiping his nose.

The Gate Patrol frogmarched them towards a sentry box under a sign reading AUTHORISED PERSONNEL ONLY.

'You know this is a Security Zone?'

'We're on our way to get Registered,' Ant said, boldly.

'Name?'

'Steven Gerrard.'

The Gate Patrol tipped back his hat. An officer appeared out of nowhere. 'I'll deal with this,' he said.

'Sir, I think this might be the Hatt boy –'

'At ease,' said the officer, tapping the Patrol once, smartly, beneath his hat. Patrol reeled and seemed to forget what he was doing.

'At ease . . . Sir.' Gate Patrol took out his Social Events timetable and began filling in fixtures for the Table Tennis Tournament. 'Anything else, Sir?'

'That's all.' The cart had been brought in behind them. The officer took Spence's bridle. He led them along a drive to a paddock filled with sheep. Securing Spencer to a tree, the strange officer turned to Ant. He took off his hat, and the light and shade under the tree dappled and played games with his face.

Now Ant recognised the man who'd helped him at the river. 'You – you lifted her into the boat,' he stumbled.

Your grandmother can stay here. The words seemed to lance into his brain. *She's got lung capacity left and the heart muscle will stand up for a while.*

'But we've got to get to hos—'

Not yet. Come with me.

In a dream Ant and Mark felt compelled to follow

the strange officer's legs through the grasses of the wild perimeter zone. In a dream, butterflies rose in front of them like glittering leaves. They walked on through an avenue of trees, and now cobalt blue butterflies shimmered on poppies, and a lark warbled overhead.

'Nice butterflies,' Ant ventured.

'Quite rare,' the officer said easily, as though leading a Wildlife Tour. 'Unearthly origins of Swarf,' he went on. 'It's a question we have to leave open, until it can be discounted.'

'That's what Dad thinks,' Mark said.

At last they were looking down over Doomhilly from the dandelion-splashed rise which fell away towards the North Installation.

'Take a seat,' the officer invited.

'We should get going –'

Take a seat.

Ant sat down in the grass, and a cloud of red-and-black cinnabar moths rose around him.

'By bypassing normal procedures, we're able to have this chat.'

Ant tried to sit up. He looked at Mark, but he seemed to be asleep.

'A chat? I haven't got time for a –'

With a movement so swift he could barely follow

it, the stranger tapped Ant's forehead and he felt as if mercury had been poured into his brain. Quicksilver images tumbled one after another through his mind, and a shifting face whispered again and again: *Something's happening. It's important young seeds understand. Something's happening . . .* The images grew fiercer and more rapid, until Ant thought his brain would burst. 'Stop!'

The flap of a moth's wing seemed to slow exquisitely, so that Ant could see every detail of its body. He watched it take an age to settle on his knee. 'Who are you?' he managed to ask.

'Nash.'

'Nash who?'

'Just Nash.'

The wind whistled between them and gusted towards the line of white radar dishes listening on the top of the hill.

'You might like to leave by the North Gate,' Nash murmured. 'Shortest way to the hospital.'

'Yes,' said Ant, 'we will.'

'We want young people to appreciate what it is that we're doing, here. Young people, especially.'

'Why me?'

Red seeds are like meteors.

'But –'

'You, and others like you, will grow up to do extraordinary things.'

'Destroying Swarf, you mean?'

Nash threw back his head, and his laughter was like a ticking clock.

'Aren't you destroying Swarf?'

Saving it.

'You're not doing tests?'

On seeds, like you.

'You spoke to me in my garden.'

Yes.

Now Ant remembered the full content of what had been passed on to him, the night the Dust fell. His brain buzzed with neon-bright lines, zipping between dimensions, worlds. 'Everything's interconnected.'

Yes.

The lines changed to climbing ropes connecting soldiers strung over a rock-face: 'But they were trying out Swarf-proof containers at the quarry –'

Pathetic attempts to halt the effect.

'Who are you?'

Not the army.

'I don't understand.'

'You don't have to. You just have to grow up,' Nash said.

The wind rushed through the poppies and rattled the

windsocks dotting the airfield. The range of laboratories looked closer now. TESTING FACILITY, read a sign. Ant tried to spot the cart. Nan was down there somewhere, tethered with Spence to a paddock fence which was probably guarding laboratory animals. Here he was, at Doomhilly – at the heart of the investigation into Swarf, and the heart of the mystery of his Seeding, *and they seemed to be the same thing*. The full force of the encounter in the garden, the night the green rain fell, flooded into his mind.

'Dogs'll be out in a minute.' Nash was scouring the airfield too, his long-fingered hands shading his eyes. 'Being near the Facility could get you into a lot of trouble – just why would you take the risk?'

'To get my Nan to hospital?'

Nash nodded. 'I've been watching you since you left.'

'Since we left Nan's house – why?'

'You're unusually resourceful. We need you, and others like you, to find a new way ahead.'

Ant's attention whirled away as the shifting face talked on about Youth being the Hope for the Future. His brain couldn't take any more. Nash rose, straightening his uniform. Ant could see now that it was the wrong colour entirely, the tabs and buttons a fuzzy match for an army officer's get-up.

Somehow Nash's influence had made everyone see it as a uniform, pulling the wool over their eyes, differently, just as the man at the river had *happened* to be there, walking his dog – 'You're the Third Agency aren't you?'

'If you like. Not from here. From far away. Caring. Sending green rain.' Nash spoke rapidly, now: 'We're defending Swarf, yes – and seeding young people with ideas for the future, all different, some big, some small. At this installation we've infiltrated the attempt to investigate Swarf, so that we can control the response.'

'Response?'

'To a pause in the rush to destruction.'

'As in pollution from cars?'

'To a pause,' Nash repeated, 'in the rush. We stop them from finding an antidote to what they call Swarf.'

All this time, Mark had seemed to be fast asleep. Ant was alone in the long grass with something he didn't understand.

'Right,' he said, uncertainly, looking around for escape.

'Red seeds are fiery. They explode into action. You won't say anything, will you?'

'About the Third Agency?' Only someone from outer space would think anything a kid said mattered. 'Not a word,' Ant promised.

'We're glad you won't let the pig out of the bag – I think that's the expression.' Nash brushed sticks off his knees with delicate flicks of his fingers.

'Cat,' said Ant.

'We're glad you won't let the pig out of the cat,' Nash practised, solemnly. *The Third Agency trusts you to make a difference, one day.*

'Yes,' Ant promised, dream-like. 'I will.'

Centring its peculiar badge with his long fingers, Nash replaced his hat. He stooped briefly, and his touch felt as cold as steel in the centre of Ant's forehead. He gave Ant a searching look that made him feel distinctly odd. The last thing Ant saw before the fuzziness behind his eyes met at the front of his head, were the long legs in their odd fake uniform striding away over the airstrip.

Ant woke from a dream about Nature Boy. He sat up and rubbed his eyes. Stu hadn't even been a big mate – why had Biggins thought that he was? Mark was the one; Mark the one he hung out with, at least until –

'Mark! Wake up!'

Mark Biggins lay on his back with his mouth open. Little black flies had died on his cheeks and shiny purple grass seeds speckled his hair. Ant made a rocket of grass seeds and fired it in Biggins's face.

Mark sat up, spluttering.

'April showers.'

'Cheers for that.' Mark spat out seeds – seeds which could spring into life, when planted and warmed, just enough, by the sun. Amazing, how precisely things were set up. Now, in the nick of time, green jelly had come from space to lock engines solid, and stop people messing up the balance. Friendly Swarf, O glorious Swarf! Ant thought he understood . . .

'What happened?' Mark got up.

'We dozed off, or something – got lost in this grass.'

'No way – what time is it, anyway?' Biggins looked at his watch.

Ant licked his lips. 'Thing is, there might be someone – some*thing* – sending Swarf.' The wind rushed up and lifted his hair, as if releasing him from his promise: 'A Third Agency, I mean. Not *us.*'

'Whatever.' Mark shivered. 'Let's walk.'

They walked as far as the avenue of trees, when Ant looked down the long perspective and stopped.

'I never hung out with Stu Diamond much, you know that, don't you? We climbed up to a buzzard's nest, once or twice. When the chicks were dead, he couldn't handle it – and I bumped into him a couple of other times, before – you know –'

'Forget it,' Mark shrugged.

'Sorry about popping you one, earlier.'

Mark rubbed his eye. 'Popped you one as well, didn't I?' And at last he grinned.

Ant wished he could forget a lot of things, but he had the feeling he'd remembered more about the secret whispers in his mind in the last ten minutes, in the long grass at Doomhilly than he had in the last four days. Now he remembered Nan.

'Which way is it?' he worried. 'Which way did we come in?'

Across the open downs, they hotfooted it back to the place they'd last seen Spence. The oak tree still watched over the paddock. The sheep still drowsed under its shade. But now Spence grazed with them, contentedly, now *inside*.

Quarantined Animal Enclosure, read the sign on the gate.

'Lab animals – *and* they've got Spence!' Ant looked for Spencer's harness – the cart – a figure! 'My nan – what have they done – where *is* she?'

Mark Biggins even looked up the tree. He squinted behind the sentry post and in the hollows beside the track.

But the red cart – and Nan – were gone.

10. Suns on the Water

'Guard dogs! Run!' Mark Biggins took off as if he'd been scalded. A couple of big hounds came bounding around the side of a warehouse, tongues lolling, gimlet eyes hungry for fugitives, their handler egging them on.

'Wait for me!' Ant careered down the nearest hill after Mark, smashing through drifts of poppies, scanning for Nan as he went – could she have wandered off? The hill swept down towards a waterway. Ant windmilled down it, tearing his legs on brambles, hurdling rocks and rabbit holes, his calves electric with danger, the leading dog's breath at his heels. In moments it would drag him down and hold him – then there'd be questions, delays . . .

He threw himself towards the canal. Over gorse and heather, mine-waste and industrial-looking rails, straight across a towpath and dark water – and into a waiting barge! Ant steadied himself. A still figure sat in the stern.

'Nan! Is that you?'

Before the figure could reply, Mark zigzagged to join them and stood teetering on the edge of the canal.

'Jump! You can make it!' But even as Ant beckoned, his momentum carried the barge away from Mark.

'Go on without me, I'll be fi—'

Ant watched helplessly as a dog felled his best friend. The handler picked him up and shook him like a rabbit.

'Don't worry,' Mark yelled. 'Dad'll sort it!'

Mark's voice faded as the barge drifted into a tunnel. *Friendship Canal* a plaque announced. *Mooring of Historic Barge* Perseverance. *Preserved by the Doomhilly Trust.*

A second dog had plunged into the canal and was pulling strongly towards them until the handler took out a whistle, and the dog turned and swam back. Ant ducked just in time. The darkness of the tunnel engulfed the barge before he could turn to quiz Nan.

Now a current running against them was posting them back out to the dog-handler. Ant's hand found a pole.

'Some disappearing act,' he scolded, angry with her for disappearing. He pushed off from the wall of the tunnel and found he could pole into the darkness ahead, unsteadily at first, then more confidently. 'Wandering off like that, where did you think you were going?'

'That's right,' Nan said, 'but walk the...pole.'

'Suppose I hadn't found you?' Ant was still cross. He tried walking the pole, all the same, and found that he could make progress by planting it and walking along the barge, planting and walking, each time crossing the old tarpaulin heaped up in the bottom. It was hard work but, bit by bit, they were entering the dim world of the canal under Morden Down. Ahead of them rings of sunlight, like little suns on the water, stretched away into the darkness. As they poled into the light, Ant looked up. Far above them heather bobbed in the round eye of sky looking down.

'Ventil...ation shaft...lovely.' Its faint breeze sent Nan's hair wandering.

Ant remembered to be cross with her: 'Why weren't you in the cart?'

'That man come.'

'Which man?'

'Man in a uniform. He...tapped me...' Nan put a hand to her forehead. 'Go down to the...water, he says. I felt better, I got up, and I...came to the boat. Sat down in it a…minute.' She snapped up her umbrella. 'Can't be doing with…these drips.'

She looked like a Victorian lady, out for a picnic on the river, Ant thought. Whatever had happened to bring her here, it didn't matter now. He poled on smoothly, and the little suns waited on the water ahead and were replaced by the next, and the next, leading them on into the depths of the tunnel like an endless string of pearls.

They entered a new ring of light, and now there were voices above. Ant brought the barge to a halt.

'. . . and now we lost him, again,' a voice said. 'They just radioed out the alert.'

'Where do they think he's headed?' a second voice asked.

'Crebberton, they think. Cottage hospital. Old woman was in a bad way.'

Ant reached for Nan's hand. But the soldiers had moved on to talk about propane: 'All very well, ordering a pack-horse loaded with gas cylinders to be taken over the hill, has *he* tried making this so-and-so move?' The sound of a slap, then a whinny.

'Why's it being sent out?'

'Sarge ordered it, for some reason. His son's been making a fuss, bawling for a balloon to be sent up to the aqueduct.'

'Why's that?'

'Top priority. Calling it Operation Tomato.'

Curiouser and curiouser still. A warm glow accompanied the news that Markie was fine, and had hooked up with his dad. Ant felt glad about that.

'Top brass are bricking it, anyway,' the second soldier went on. 'Imposter calling himself Nash makes a monkey of 'em, not going to like it much, are they?'

'No one named Nash ever worked at HQ?'

'Total stranger. Kitted out with pips and everything. Penetrated the Testing Facility and no one said so much as a dickey-bird.'

'How'd he manage that?'

'*Wouldn't* they like to know . . .'

Ant strained to hear more, but the voices were moving away amidst the thump of horse's hooves.

'Nash...that was his name. He comes up to the... cart,' Nan murmured. 'You feel better...now, he says. Go down to the...water, he says. I found the boat. Got in it. I don't feel so...marvellous, now.'

'Shush, now,' Ant told her. Nan's fingers were blue, he could see. He pictured reaching Intensive Care, handing her over, the massive relief. He leaned on his pole and set them moving, crossing and re-crossing the tarp in the bottom of the barge with every shove and reach.

91

The next shaft gave him a second good look at her. Nan's face had darkened with the effort of breathing. The current rippled past and tried to pull them back, and the little suns stretched away into the unending darkness ahead, and there was no way of knowing how long it went on, where or if the tunnel ever came out above Crebberton or – worst of all thoughts – even if its entrance was blocked.

Ant searched his memory of Crebberton. The canal ran along beside the school and disappeared into a hillside, he supposed, somewhere off the road towards the town tip. His mind flitted over the landscape, trying to penetrate its secrets. Suddenly remembering where the mouth of the tunnel was seemed more important than his next heartbeat.

Anthony Granville Hatt poled on, thinking deeply. Darkness enclosed the slim barge as it crept under Morden Down, and only the tinkle of the current and the occasional ring of light on the water let him know that they weren't buried alive.

Poor Spence, they'd rescue him later. Poor Mark, left behind to face the music. Poor Billy, lost along the way. Ant had fallen into a rhythm with his pole. Poor Spence, poor Mark, poor Nan –

'Poor Mister Balrog.'

Ant froze. 'Who's there?' Drips from the roof answered him and the current rustled past, as usual.

'Didn't think you'd lost me, did you?' A hand grasped Ant's leg, and he leapt in terror. Another hand grasped his pole. Immediately the bow drifted round and locked the barge across the canal.

'Not very good at this, are you?' the voice gloated. Then the pole was shoved back at him. 'Carry on with it, then, or we'll never get out of here.'

The horrible presence of Balrog! Balrog here, all along burst into Ant's mind. He straightened *Perseverance* with an effort. He pushed off against stonework he couldn't see and poled on, heart hammering, aiming for the next ring of light.

'Give it some welly, then.'

Ant redoubled his efforts, the barge nosed into the light, and the vent shaft showed him the white face and the black coat, the shape of his worst nightmares, lounging in the stern.

'You look like you got smacked in the gob with a wet fish,' the "blind" man sneered.

'Where did *you* come from?'

'Kipping under the tarp, wasn't I, till your clumping woke me up.' Balrog patted the tarpaulin Ant had clambered over a hundred times.

'Hiding, you mean, till there was no way back.'

'You wasn't very kind to a blind man, before.'
Balrog laughed unpleasantly and stretched his
legs towards Nan. 'Plenty of room, now, isn't that
right, Missus?'

Nan brought out her umbrella.

'None of that, or we'll fall out,' Balrog threw it over
the side.

'Soldiers everywhere,' said Ant, to distract him.
'Funny you didn't get picked up.'

Balrog grunted. 'I did, but I gave 'em the slip.'

'They're looking for us, aren't they – me and Nan?'
Ant tested him, picturing Balrog's gaze sweeping
the bushes at Heartsease Cross, his readiness to
betray them.

'Looking for everyone who gets over the river.
Poor Mister Balrog, he just wants a ride to town, he
wouldn't cross the road to help that martial law lot,'
he went on, secure in his lie. 'He only wants to get to
Crebberton.'

'Why, is your family there?'

'General Registration, haven't you heard?'

'For petrol rations or something?'

'Ha. Ha. That's the runaround. Want to get
Registered where there's food depots, don't you? Buy
up as much as you can, sell on to other areas, fortune
to be made.'

So that was it. In the scramble to survive in the Days After The Dust, Balrog's would be the foot in the old person's, or the child's, face, the one to hoard bread and milk. Ant shrank past him to reach the stern. A plastic bag caught on his pole. He shook it off in disgust.

'Catching a crab?' Balrog jeered. 'Step on it, will you? We haven't got all day.'

'Get away from him, I...say!'

Ant turned. Something gleamed in Nan's hand.

'Now, Missus, we *won't* fall out.' Balrog put his hands up. The barge rocked as he scrambled away and they entered the ring of light Nan had been waiting for.

'Up the other...end, now! All right...sit down.'

'Nan! Where did you get that gun?'

'Fred gave it to me, 'case of..burg-u-lars.' She waved the antique weapon at Balrog. 'Put him under that... sack, that'll damp...'im down.'

Ant pulled a sack from the bottom of the barge and covered Balrog's head. He really was blind, now.

'Twenty notes, if you get me out of this,' he hissed.

Ant shut him up with a push. 'So Fred lent you a gun.' He was certain the old gun didn't work.

'Thinks a lot of me...he does. Not called...Kitty Hamley for nothing, he...named his...engine for me.'

'But your name's Katherine.'

'Kitty, he called me. Engaged we were, till he started rebuildin'...that engine, so I...married George Ball instead...'

Grandpa Ball had died when Ant was little. He thought he remembered the smell of a jacket, a pair of knees by the fire –

'...but not soon enough, and...the fact is, Fred's your grandfather.'

'*What*? What did you say?'

'Poor Mister Balrog, he can't breathe in here,' the sack whined. 'Nan got any eatables, has she?'

'What d'you mean "Fred"?' Ant asked Nan, harshly. 'How d'you *mean* he's my grandfather?'

'Don't ask me now...Anthony...'

'When's someone going to let me out?' The sack stood up and wobbled. 'This tunnel's four kilometres long.'

'What's at the end of it?' Ant demanded. 'Where does it come out, in Crebberton?'

'Let me out and I'll tell you.'

'You don't know anything.'

'Try me.'

'Fall out and drown, I don't care.' Ant hardly recognised his own voice. Nan had fallen back, exhausted. Ant felt like shaking her – asking her what she meant by telling him bizarre things about his grandfather while they were stuck in a tunnel. 'Does Mum know?'

'She does...now, I'm telling you 'case we...don't get to...hospital.'

Ant took up his pole again. No one else was going to. 'Tell you a story, if you like.'

'Anthony, I know...it's a...shock...'

'People think I didn't know Stu Diamond – I did, I knew him, a bit.' You could say anything you wanted in the darkness under Morden Down. Nan could say gross things about Fred. He, Ant, could say things he'd never dreamed he'd say to anyone in the darkness of the tunnel, and no one would ever hear them again. Anything could go out into that tunnel and be buried forever under Morden Down.

'We climbed up to check a buzzard's nest once, but when we got there, the chicks were dead. He found things like that hard to take, he – he kept saying he didn't fit in, he heard voices telling him something would change, he'd be a part of it –' Ant cleared his throat. 'So then, *that* day, the day it happened, it's windy, and Biggins and me are up on the hill flying his fighting kite, and Mark goes, "That's Stu, that is" – up on the Point – "he's never going to jump from the top."'

Ant's voice rolled around in the tunnel. Even the sack sat down and inclined itself to listen.

'So Markie crashes the kite, and I have to go up to the Point. He's there, all right – Nature Boy, right on the edge. "What are you doing, you dufus," I'm asking him. "Tombstoning," he says. "*No one* jumps from here," I'm going – and they're all below, shouting, "No!"' Ant walked back with his pole, and his knuckles were white as he gripped it. '"I want to fit in," he goes. "I'll show 'em I can do it." He's wobbling on the edge, and the wind's blowing like mad, and *I know I'm not near enough to grab him.*'

Ant poled two whole strokes before he spoke again. '"Don't be stupid," I'm going, "there's years of twitching ahead of you, who's gonna watch the birds?" The lake's like, a million miles below, and he squats down his legs to jump. "The world's messed up, I'm lonely," he goes, and he looks at me, and he's gone. Then there's a clap on the water, and they're all rushing around like ants – and I never talked him down, and some people think he *jumped* because of me and my mouth. I never said anything to make him, but I never said anything to *stop* him –'

'Anthony,' said Nan. 'Stop...'

'I never told the investigation. Me and Markie kept

out of it. Stu was a second cousin of Kim's and now Kim's gone and dumped him, Markie that is, 'cos she's annoyed he never told her how I was up there with him – Nature Boy – before –'

Nan reached for him. 'There,' she said. 'It's all...right.'

'You can't hug me, I'm poling. I get my mouth from Mum,' Ant went on, 'and I called him a freak and a geek. I should've been more sympathetic, then he might've had *one* mate at least –'

Nan's chest worked as though it would burst. 'Anthony...don't...upset yourself...'

'Nan,' Ant sobbed, 'hang on, I'm going to help you.'

Now, as if it mattered, his secret was in the water, the bricks, the vault of the roof – in Balrog, and in Nan, and the echoes in the tunnel had absorbed it, and would keep it to themselves. He pushed on in desperation until at last his pole dragged and he was making no progress at all. He secured the barge across the canal and lay down, and it seemed to him that they slept.

I can't ring, I'm in a tunnel – Dad, please, I've got no signal – Ant sat up suddenly. A drip from the roof hit him squarely in the centre of his head. It felt like a tap from Nash. He picked up his pole and got going. The darkness in front of him had shaded to grey. They must've slept for ages. A long time seemed to have passed.

A warm breeze lifted Ant's hair. A smack of morning was in the air. Somewhere not too far away, a new day was dawning. Nan and Balrog made lumps in the greying light. Ant walked to and fro past them. At last the sack stirred and sat up.

'Morning.'

'Is it?' the sack asked. It thought a bit. 'Funny customer, Nash.'

'You know Nash?'

'Gave me a grilling about you, didn't he?'

'He did?' Ant tried to imagine it. 'What did he want to know?'

'How you treated me.'

'And?'

'Had to tell him, didn't I?'

Images from the mad dash downhill seemed to pop up in front of him – Ant saw again the white hand on the cart, the arms clawing their way up, the frantic pleas of the "blind" man, Nan beating him off – himself, Ant, screaming at him to go. *All human beings, aren't we?* Balrog had wheedled, at the bridge. Now Ant felt ashamed of himself. They'd held a man in a sack for hours. What must it have been like? In a moment he felt he was Balrog, hungry, thirsty, cold, afraid. In the same moment he rose, and tore off the sack. Poor Mister Balrog rubbed his head. He hugged his long black coat and nursed his elbows.

Ant took out his last bottle of water. 'You must be thirsty.'

'You guessed it.' Balrog drank deep and ate the biscuits Ant proffered. 'Don't mind if I do.'

'Funny how our paths keep crossing.'

'Funny,' said Balrog. 'Ha, ha.'

'You knew we were in the bushes at Heartsease Cross – you could see exactly where we were – why didn't you give us away?'

'Going to, wasn't I, till *he* stopped me.'

'Who?'

'Him,' said Balrog, simply.

Ant turned, and the end of the tunnel blazed with dawning light. Nash waited, silhouetted against it.

'You villain,' he said, 'that'll do.'

Ant looked at Balrog – he didn't feel heroic himself – who was the villain? He waited gravely for Nash to pick them up and solve every puzzle he'd been through. Balrog started up. Jumping out of the barge, he floundered down the canal and made a dash for the tunnel mouth. He dodged under Nash's arm, and Nash let him go. The dark figure flailed out of the tunnel and dropped away, and the morning light blazed in more brightly still, and welcomed Ant into a new day.

Ant held his breath as the barge carried him out under the disappearing stars, and a glorious dawn opened over him, and the roof of the tunnel fell away under a sparkling morning sky. A fresh breeze bathed his face and body. Below lay fields, woods, a town tinted pink in the rising sun. The Friendship Canal ran on over a towering aqueduct flashed with red and gold.

Nash made a flourish as if to say, *All this is yours.* It seemed to Ant that he stood beside him, and together they watched Balrog pitching and sliding down the slope and escaping across the fields like a wild man – like a prehistoric man flailing back into time.

'What shall we do with him?' Nash smiled.

Ant felt sorry for him. 'He's all right – let him go.'

It seemed to him that Nash enfolded him in a dark cloak, and his mind drifted free over the world. Nash, Balrog, himself, who was he? As a fiery dawn broke over Crebberton, Ant wasn't sure any more.

11. The Third Agency

Light and darkness flashed past him. Questions tumbled like odd socks in his brain and he was struggling against some sort of boundary, holding him close. One thing he had to know: 'Why are you watching me? What's going on? You helped me at the river –'

At the river – and other places. Nash's voice hissed in Ant's mind.

'Why?'

You know, by now, the answer came.

'You put things in my way.'

To see what you'd do.

'You made me fall asleep in the long grass.'

To show you why.

'You told Nan to find the barge.'

To help you on your way.

'You sent me Balrog.'

To show you yourself.

The answers beat about him like a storm. Enormous pressures shifted around him. Ant drew close and the winds whistled through Nash's dark cloak. Still he fought to free himself, and below him clouds seemed to part and he saw Mark and his father, heard their voices:

'You know the trouble you've got me in?' the Sergeant demanded. 'What am I supposed to do, now?'

'I don't know,' Mark said. 'I'm sorry.'

Nash flourished his dark cloak and the scene changed – Doomhilly this time.

'What do you know about Anthony's state of mind?' Sergeant Biggins closed the door of the interview room.

'His Nan's dying, what do you think?'

'You know he's with a dangerous man?'

Mark looked at his father. 'What d'you mean?'

'A dangerous fugitive calling himself Mr Balrog was seen climbing into the barge. We've put a watch on the tunnel-mouth – what?'

Mark began to laugh. 'The Balrog's a monster from Lord of the Rings. Someone's winding you up.'

The four winds pressed about him, and Ant saw the scene moving on:

'...and no one named Nash has ever worked here.' Sergeant Biggins put away a checklist.

'We saw him,' said Mark. 'He was an officer.'

'An imposter – trying to sabotage the Facility. These are extraordinary times, Mark. You'd be better off at home.'

'You don't know that he's attacking the Facility – he might be trying to help.'

'Help? How?'

'There's a Third Agency, Anthony said. Stopping pollution on Earth.'

'Visitors from outer space?'

'The green stuff's got to come from somewhere.'

'Why would they send Swarf?'

'Gum things up? Give us time to think?' Mark shrugged. 'Because they can?'

Sergeant Biggins frowned: 'What's got into you lately? Now Kim tells me you were up on the hill, the day that lad drowned in the lake.'

Mark jumped up. 'That doesn't matter now. Did you order the propane yet?'

'I told you – it's on its way.' Sergeant Biggins looked at his son with respect. 'Concerned about them, aren't you?'

'Ant's my mate, what do you think?'

Sergeant Biggins reached for the phone: 'Sally, just checking – did we send propane to the Emergency Balloon? The Crebberton area. By pack-horse. All correct? Very good.'

Nash's cloak swirled and Ant was content to be protected while new scenes whorled beneath him, too fast for his mind to take in. A thread which was Nature Boy ran through all of them, and it wasn't all right, it would never be all right, while Stu's dark thread ran through recent scenes like a flaw:

'Why are you testing me?'

You, and other red seeds.

Beneath Ant the clouds parted again and Nature Boy fleetingly took off his ever-present hat, and the light glanced off his red hair. A tomato – of course – like himself! 'Called Stu too early, did you?' Ant accused Nash, angrily. 'He heard voices, he didn't understand – *you* mixed him up and he topped himself!'

No.

'He thought he was different – he *was* different –'

Listen to me –

'Leave me alone, let me go!'

Nash flared his cloak in anger and it seemed to Ant that a thundercloud rolled up, engulfing them inside it. The rosy dawn, the valley, the woods and the town were gone, and a green world opened in front of him under Nash's cape, and they were flying over a green desert, in a haze of green, under a wide green sky. Tremendous green dunes rippled under them, their angles sharp as knives.

Is everything green in your world? Ant thought that he asked Nash.

Not in my world – yours. Nash sped on, the desert dunes writhed under him and Ant felt he was drowning.

Slower! What am I, the Snowman?

Nash laughed, and showed him the desert edges creeping forward, and towns ringed with cracked mud, and towns without firewood, with no trees for many hundreds of kilometres.

The Green Kalahari – with meerkats!

Now scattering animals whirled under him in a thunderstorm, and the lightning forked down to smash a tree overlooking a farm, and the farmer rushed out, and his children.

Now they were swooping up Africa, faster than an email could travel, and it seemed to Ant that his mind fainted under the weight of the images that howled under Nash's cloak. Mountains, plains, seas, rushed by him, and now they were higher still, as though in a plane, looking down on green Europe. Now they were flying over retreating glaciers, and snowy solitudes where dark circles showed where the snow had gone. Now he was over green England, and cars teemed over it like ants.

How long d'you think this can go on?

'Go on?'

Cars – people – pressure –

'I don't know. I don't care – do I?'

I think you do. Nash rubbed his long fingers together – *shall we?*

Ant looked down at his hands and green dust welled up between his fingers and he shook it down over the valley, his village, his house, and he saw himself rushing out, falling down, Nash tapping his forehead, filling his mind with information. The scene moved on and he shook dust over the quarry, the lake. Retreating time howled under Nash's cloak, and the wind battered the hill. Two months shrank into themselves, flowers wagged and trees stooped, and a lonely figure stood on the topmost pinnacle of the hill – *Stu!*

'Get back!' Nature Boy turned. 'Leave me alone.'

Ant found a kite in his hand. He flung it down. 'No one jumps from here – what are you trying to *do*?'

'I'll show them I can fit in.' Once again the wind whistled between them, and far below wet-suited figures looked up in horror from the lake.

'See? They don't want you to jump –'

'I'm wrong,' Stu said, 'like that rabbit.'

Pictures of Ant's meetings with Nature Boy flashed by – the myxie rabbit, the squashed badger, the wilting buzzard chicks starving after their mother had been hit by a car.

'I'm lonely, the world's messed up.' Stu stood poised on the edge.

'Don't jump!' Ant struggled to reach through the green tunnel of clouds he was somehow privileged to look down through. Now he could clearly see the fridges and bicycles clogging the depths of the lake. *Don't jump, you'll mess it up even more!*

It was the only kind of appeal likely to reach him. Stu actually turned to look at Ant – in turning; stumbled – then the wind gusted up and tore him off The Point like a rag.

And in that moment looking down, Ant saw that Stu *had* hesitated, had meant to turn back. And he saw at last that it wasn't his fault – that Stu, the boy he barely knew, hadn't jumped at all and that the wind had blown him.

I was like him, Nash indicated. *Collecting animals.*

His eyes met Ant's, and a series of unimaginable creatures and strange textures criss-crossed his brain. *Can't imagine you as a kid,* Ant thought, rather than said.

Ah, then I'll show you.

Ant looked down as if from a great height, and Child Nash appeared below him very briefly as a collection of glowing lines, indescribably strange.

Your world – is Swarf in it?

Nash shook his head. *Your time and place. Nothing to do with mine.*

The green rush of past time had gone, and the colour of present time was normal, and the smell of it was home. They whirled over the moor and over a cottage surrounded with tanks and equipment. A man looked up over his hoses, and the man was Nash. Around him stood drums of chemicals and a fierce gas flame burned something off. They dipped over a town, and a woman looked up, and a man dropped his paper, and redheads crowded below –

My Nan calls redheads 'Tomatoes'.

I like that. Nash laughed. *Plants for the future. Tomato seeds.*

– and faces milled in the main street staring up, and it seemed to Ant that Nash looked out of every one of them. At last his cloak fluttered and fell. Below them a tree-lined canal looped around a valley in the lee of a moorland town. A barge waited under the trees, and in it lay a still figure, like the Lady of Shalott.

Now he was over the trees – now he was in the barge, beside her.

'Nan – we're almost in Crebberton, We're almost at the hospital!' Ant cried. 'Nan, you've got to wake up!'

12. Operation Tomato

'Nan – wake up!' Ant shook her. Nash and the four winds were gone, and at the end of the last loop in the river, near but far, the town waited, with its hospital on the hill. 'Nan – please – he *said* you could make it . . .'

'See the...'ospital, can you?' Her breath was less than a whisper.

'There – see?' Ant supported her while she glimpsed the red, fluted chimneys of the Victorian Cottage Hospital over the tops of the trees. She coughed and Ant laid her back.

'We'll soon be there.'

'What...time?'

'About ten,' Ant improvised.

'All right, m'love...'

She'd given up, Ant could see. Now a last hidden valley lay between Nan and a ventilator. He held the last of the water to her lips, but it ran away over her chin. Her lungs were pumping with what little space they had left.

He put down his head. '*Nan* . . .'

She looked at him with Nash in her eyes, and Ant had the strangest feeling. He splashed his face in the river, and it was his grandmother looking at him again, relying on him to come up with something.

Nash had gone, Balrog had gone, they were on their own again. He felt tired – tired of thinking things out, tired of having no fun, no life, no home, no mates, parents, telly. That life was so over, he could hardly remember it, now.

Once again he scanned ahead, looking for problems, ways round them. The current had eased around a passing place, Ant barely touched with his pole and the barge glided smoothly on. They slid past heaps of pink mine-waste, weathered into shapes of old men. A miners' rubbish dump mouldered under a tree. Out of it poked a boot, a cooking pot, a bottle.

'Ring...Dad?'

'Network's down. Cook at the Satellite Café said landlines are down, as well. Anyway, he never rang *me*.'

Now they were gliding between mortared embankments, and Ant saw that it was an aqueduct, and that they were crossing the valley. At the end of it they made a sharp turn. A sluice-gate dark with slime barred the way ahead. The barge ran up to it and nudged it. Ant got out. Even before he touched its rusted handle, he knew that it spelled the end for *Perseverance*.

'We'll have to get out,' he said. 'Find another way into town.'

'Things'll be normal...'gain, and you'll be back off to...school in...no time...'

'Nan –'

She was making an enormous effort to speak to him. 'This Swarf muck, it...won't hang about, and you c'n tell...your mum...about Fred.'

Ant felt sick.

'You're like her, and...*him*.'

Ant turned. Voices flickered on the wind funnelling up the valley.

He took Nan's arm. 'Look!'

Something unimaginably huge and red rose beyond the trees ahead. Voices shouted warnings about wind speed and direction of take-off. A team of men in red sweaters hung off ropes and a basket.

'No way – !' Ant's heart was in his mouth as its shadow fell over them.

The hot-air balloon strained on its ropes like the

largest tomato in the world. Its canopy read DAY OF YOUR DREAMS. Over that had been strung a banner: EMERGENCY MEDICAL BALLOON.

'Envelope full!'

'Check!'

Purple, blue and yellow flames roared into the envelope, or canopy. The balloon towered over his head like a cathedral. Ant waited beside Nan with the team.

The pilot turned down the burners. 'Flying wires free?'

'Check!' yelled the flying wires checker.

'Passengers,' the pilot beckoned, and four men wearing sweaters reading *Take Off & Recovery Crew* posted Nan into the basket, and Ant scrambled in after her.

The pilot secured her gloves. 'Been in a balloon before?'

'I have,' said Nan. Ant looked at her. Nan was full of surprises.

'In that case, you'll know that we have to hold on and brace ourselves when landing. Welcome to your airlift to hospital. Name of this balloon's *Ariel*. The wind's in the right direction, so this should be a short flight. Nice to get airborne again, now the army's come through with propane – we need a bit of grunt, to make us lighter than air.' She patted the tanks under the burner nozzles.

'Why are we lighter than air?' Ant asked.

'Because we've heated the air in the envelope, and hot air rises.'

'Why?'

'Because the molecules in hot air dash around and occupy more space, making it less dense than the air outside the balloon – you always this precise?'

'I'm not precise, I'm accurate,' said Ant.

'Weight on the basket, please!'

A gust of wind took the envelope and dragged the team along.

'Crown line fastened?'

'Check!' The crown line checker raced to secure his line.

'Everything ready? Hold on!'

The pilot gripped the burner nozzles and let out a fierce gout of flame. The mile-high envelope above him wavered – the basket leapt – they were off! In moments the ground rushed away and the waving ground crew were left behind as moving red specks in a field. Another spurt of flame, and *Ariel* and her basket rose grandly into the air, and the valley dropped away more rapidly, the woods and fields blending together faster than Ant could notice details.

Nan gripped the basket. 'My...life!'

Ant held her. 'All right? See the towpath, down there? And the barge?'

Nan saw it.

'Don't need to worry about it, now, do we?' Ant felt almost happy. It had been a job, getting this far. The Day Of Your Dreams balloon crew had explained that propane had been sent by packhorse. As Ant had been listening, a soldier had emerged from the trees and had asked him if they'd seen Balrog. His voice had been unsettlingly familiar, until Ant remembered where he'd heard it before – under the vent shaft, in the tunnel, complaining about taking propane over the hill *because the Sarge's son had been bawling about sending a balloon.*

Good old Markie. 'Balrog? Haven't seen him,' Ant had told the patrol. 'Not since he ran away.'

The soldier made a note and marched off.

'Hamper, here,' the pilot said, pushing it out with her foot.

Strawberries, chocolates and cider! Ant opened a note in astonishment. 'Balloon & hamper, compliments of Sergeant Biggins.' *Get well soon,* he'd added, in his own handwriting. *An emergency makes us more human, not less – sorry for not helping earlier.*

Ant handed a drink to the pilot. The wind

freshened beneath them and hurried them across the sky – soon they'd go bumping from cloud to cloud, like Nan feared, when she was four. Another gout of flame from the burners, and *Ariel* spurred on with the wind, and the valley spun underneath and the moor opened out beyond, and Crebberton grew sharper, and more distinct, on the side of its hill.

'Good lift, today,' said the pilot.

And now the earth showed Ant its edges like a great bowl of salad, a bowl that contained everything that was worth having or caring about, and it wasn't so big, after all.

'Never dreamed I'd...see this.'

Ant squeezed Nan's hand. 'Hold on.'

For an answer, she opened her bag, and Ant took out the antique pistol Fred had lent her, and dropped it over the side of the basket into the river. Together, they watched it flash away. They watched the river switching away to the sea. Towards the horizon seagulls wheeled and yachts bent their sails in the sunlight.

The burners hadn't roared for a while. Beneath him Crebberton looked close enough to touch and it seemed to Ant that they were losing height. He pointed out the hospital in its patchwork of grounds. Now he was certain they were lower. 'You'll be comfy, soon.'

'Yes...' Nan whitened as they came in.

'This is Lifeline Balloon Tango-Bravo-Tango calling Crebberton General.' The pilot spoke to the Emergency Room over her radio. 'Clear landing space. Coming in with a suspected heart failure, female, eighty-five.'

Female heart failure, eighty-five – it didn't sound much like Kitty Hamley, gunslinger and grandmother with a secret, who'd survived a runaway cart, a jump from an ore-wagon, a journey under Doomhilly. Now Ant could pick out the tennis court behind the hospital. They'd marked a cross with white sheets.

'It's a bit hit-and-miss!' the pilot yelled. 'We'll come in as near as we can!'

It was then that Ant noticed the clouds blowing in from the West. He pointed over Nan's head at the green thunderheads rolling in rapidly behind them.

'No way – green clouds!'

The pilot stared. 'Strange formations.'

A shining green column marched under the clouds.

'Unreal,' said Ant. *Green rain!*

The same wind that brought the green rain whirled *Ariel* towards her destination. In moments the column slammed into them. Ant threw back his head to meet it, and the rain beat over him and green dust coated the basket, the burners, the fuel tanks, frosting Nan's hair with green and topping the pilot's strawberries.

The column of rain swept over them, and marched on. Ant craned out of the basket as everywhere, floods joined the rain. He watched, dumbstruck, as green streams of Swarf gushed from wrecked filling stations, changing back into petrol before they'd reached the road.

Ant's mobile rang. 'Dad? A hot air balloon – everywhere, it's amazing –' His jaw dropped, he couldn't stop looking. For the first time in his life, Anthony Hatt was speechless.

The green dust swept the landscape and in every place it had passed, Swarf became petrol again. Ant squinted into the far distance behind it, and something flashed in the sun – a myriad of car roofs, crossing and meeting in the lanes, cars flooding out onto the roads!

It was an incredible sight.

Shapes moved beneath him now. Someone in the middle of Crebberton tried their ignition, and a few streets away a furniture van shuddered to life. In minutes the town square smoked with drivers trying their engines and sounding their horns in triumph. The fire brigade rode out, shouting warnings about petrol in the road. The Big Wheel in the fairground began to turn, slowly at first, then faster. Across town an ambulance wailed, and a familiar black Golf followed it up the hill to the hospital.

'Dad? Unbelievable – I can see you!' Ant waved his mobile. 'How did you know where we were going?'

'Worked it out.' A hand sprouted out of the car below. His father tooted. 'We can see you, too!'

No way could anyone miss the monster red balloon coming down over the hospital, like some kind of mother-craft. In the town centre shoppers stared, and red-headed kids at the Leisure Centre came wonderingly out in their swimming costumes. In the town square other young Tomatoes stood waiting, red seeds, all of them. A wedding with an auburn-haired bridesmaid came rushing out of the church and stood staring up at the balloon.

Ant hung over the basket and waved. He was coming to join them, in the biggest tomato of all!

Miles away over the moor, Nash pushed back his hat and watched the red balloon set over the hospital like a sun. When it had disappeared, he carried on filtering cooking oil into a drum and the wind whistled through his long fingers as he set it over a fire.

'Brace for landing!' the pilot cried.

Now the wind had died completely, and they

were floating down in the stillness left behind the column of green rain. The reception committee milled around below but, strangely, no one spoke. Only the sound of the basket creaking beneath his feet as he braced himself behind Nan told Ant they were about to touch down. He could even hear the pilot's breathing, as gently and vertically in the centre of the crossed sheets, they touched – bounced – touched again, and many hands closed on *Ariel's* basket. The pilot pulled the parachute cord to let hot air out of the envelope. Gently, like a collapsing giraffe, the balloon lay down over the tennis court.

'Textbook,' said the pilot, taking off her gloves.

Waiting arms passed Nan onto a gurney and hurried her away. Ant watched her hand, raised in a wave to him, disappearing under the sign saying IN PATIENTS.

'Woke up at Connor's farm at five, this morning,' his mobile burst into life again.

'Dad?'

'Of course, we came home, right away – Neil Griffith's mother said she'd heard you were on your way to hospital – Crebberton, we supposed –'

Ant waved across the car park.

'We set off to find you then we saw the balloon –'

Ant's mother climbed out of the car and waved – then his father, ear to his phone.

'Missed you, Dad,' Ant told his mobile.

'We rang and rang – the network was down – and we missed you so much, and you can have enough of getting up to milk cows at six o'clock in the morning –'

Ant grinned. No kidding. Now he saw his dad.

'Aren't *you* a sight for sore eyes.' Ant's father dropped his mobile and strode towards his son. He put out his arms, and waited, and Ant flung himself towards them.

13. Nan's Journey

Across the world, Swarf had morphed back into petrol. As mysteriously as it had arrived, the dust that had triggered the change had reversed it again, and the green jelly was history. Samples preserved in museums melted into stains, and even neighbour Neil Griffiths' Peugeot coughed into life and smoked around the village again. He even washed the bird-droppings off it one Saturday morning, flicking suds over the hedge as he did it. Ant flicked water back. In no time a war of buckets broke out, until Neil threw down his sponge. 'Thanks for soaking me, Hatt.'

'How old are you, anyway?'

'Eighteen, how *old* are you?'

Dad was watching the lunchtime news, but he looked up as Ant came in. 'Just a bit wet, then.'

'What's new?' Ant nodded at the telly.

'Swarf, the post-mortem, as usual.'

The usual scientists were rushing to explain that they had understood that Swarf was a "temporary phenomenon", all along. The atmosphere of the Earth had been hostile to the green jelly that everyone shrugged off as a joke, it had always been hostile, it had only been a matter of time until Swarf melted away. There had never been any danger of a collapse of services. Analysis of Swarf had revealed that there had been no permanent threat. A spokeswoman from Doomhilly was ready to comment.

Ant listened impatiently. The spokeswoman's name was Mary Gandalf. Her long fingers flickered over her pockets as she spoke. While the Swarf lockup had been a temporary nuisance, it had, she said, highlighted the need for a change to alternative fuels. Things might as well change, before they *had* to.

'Forward thinking for you,' Dad said, sardonically.

'Don't think she's *real*, do you?' Ant could see through her right away. She had Third Agency written through her like a stick of rock.

'How d'you mean, real?'

'How many people are called "Gandalf"?'

Dad thought about it. 'Pass us an apple,' he said, crunching into it cheerfully.

Fresh food transported around the countryside by jolly truck-drivers was still a novelty in the days after the un-swarfing. Still the Village Hall Committee had been talking about growing apples again in Minnow's Orchard. Everyone would have a stake with a few trees. If and when Swarf came again, they could whistle for apples upcountry, *we'd* be all right, Jack – that was how his father had put it to the committee, and Ant could see it made sense.

School had been back for a while, which made Saturdays worth their weight. Later Ant took his skateboard up to Spencer's field, and put his chin on the gate: 'All right, you old slug?'

Spence ambled over immediately and nosed up the mints Ant offered.

'You'll rot his teeth.'

'Sorry?'

'Thanks for making him move.' Kim Diamond stepped out from behind the horse, curry comb in hand. 'Trying to groom him, aren't I?'

Ant hadn't seen Mark's ex since the two-month anniversary of her cousin's death, at the quarry. 'How come you're grooming Spence?'

'Since Fred bought him from his neighbour, and asked me?'

'When did Fred buy him?'

'Mark drove the cart back from Doomhilly. Fred liked the look of him –'

The mention of Biggins made both of them uncomfortable.

'– though he isn't a carthorse,' Kim finished. 'And Fred just collected carts. But now we might take him to shows.'

Ant tore up a handful of long grass and balanced it across Spencer's nose. In moments, the grey tongue rolled up and folded it into his mouth.

Kim laughed. 'When'd you teach him that?'

'Taught himself, didn't he?' Ant patted the chestnut fondly. 'Smart horse, cool name – Mark's dad got him out of the compound at Doomhilly or he might've ended up in a test tube,' Ant joked.

'I heard.'

'About Stu – I know I was the last one to see him, and I should've told you about it –'

Kim began currying Spence vigorously.

'The thing is, it was an accident. He didn't jump, he fell.'

Kim changed sides and began on Spencer's flanks.

'He started to come towards me, see, but the wind blew him back, and – thing is, I blanked it out because he'd said something about topping himself once, and I felt bad I didn't stop him –'

'Poor you,' Kim said.

'It was an accident,' Ant repeated slowly. 'Stu cared

about animals too much to mess up, big time.'

The curry comb described big circles and finally stopped. 'He had posters of hawks on his bedroom walls.' Kim remembered. 'He loved hawks – raptors he called them.'

'Raptors,' Ant nodded. 'That's right.'

'I know.'

Kim put Spencer's hoof between her knees and began cleaning it out with a penknife attachment.

'It wasn't Mark's fault he never mentioned we were there. I made him promise not to tell –'

'How's your Nan?' Kim asked.

Ant swallowed. 'Responding to medication.'

'When are you visiting?'

'This avo.'

Kim nodded. 'Can I visit with Mark?'

There'd been so much to catch up with since the second wave of green rain had washed over Uncle Connor's farm at five o'clock in the morning, unswarfing the generator and sending the milking machine mad. The lights in the yard had blazed down over the sleeping cattle and a corn grinder in the barn had taken up where it had left off with a din like the town band falling downstairs.

When Connor and Ant's parents had bumped

into each other turning everything off, they'd tried Connor's car and he'd driven Ant's parents home. They'd met Neil Griffiths' mother at the door with Midge the cat in her arms. As she was telling them there was an alert out for a boy in a cart, trying to get through to the hospital, green rain had washed over Dad's car. Ant knew the rest, but it didn't help him to understand the whole thing. A Tomato like other Tomatoes, just what had his Seeding been *for*?

Visiting time again. Now that everything had come unswarfed, ranks of busy ambulances waited outside the Hospital. Ant's mother pulled into the car park and turned off the engine.

'You can go in and say hello – I'm just slipping down to the shops for a couple of things for Nan.'

Ant didn't feel like getting out. The same journey to Crebberton General that had been written in blood in his heart during the Swarfing had taken them thirty-five minutes by car. Already the flowers at Heartsease Cross flashed by as though they were a smudge in the hedge.

'What?' Ant paused. His mother had something to say.

'Something I should've told you. Well, there's no easy way. I – knew about Nan and Fred.'

Ant looked at her. 'Since when?'

'Since only a little while ago. I think Nan was getting things off her chest. I was looking for a time to tell you, then we got Swarfed, and – well, time slipped by –'

'Weren't you angry not to know who your real dad was?'

'As far as I'm concerned, George – Grandpa Ball was my dad.'

Ant had never really known him. 'Must be weird, I suppose.'

'It's different for you, of course –'

Ant got out of the car.

'You're like him, you know. Fred had red hair, Nan says. You saved her,' Ant's mum said. 'You handled things – and I haven't thanked you for that.'

'Could've *told* me Fred Salter was my grandfather.' It seemed weird to say it, now.

'We can talk more, if you'd like.'

Ant thought. 'Does Fred know?'

'Just. Tell Nan I'll be in to see her, in half an hour.'

Ant watched his mother drive off, wondering why she couldn't've left the car, and walked down to do her shopping. Amazing how strongly he felt about unnecessary car journeys these days.

Mark and Kim were waiting hand-in-hand in Reception. Mark looked sheepish: 'Yo.'

Upstairs in Renfrew Ward, for a surprise, they found Fred Salter beside Nan's bed.

He jumped up, hat in hand. 'Here's trouble.'

'Anthony?' Nan flushed with pleasure. 'Now, then,' she told Fred, 'you don't have to go.'

'Two visitors at time, I'm outnumbered.' He screwed on his cap. 'Kim. Mark – Anthony.' His horny engineer's hands were shaking as he said cheerio. Ant found himself studying the fluff under his hat for any signs of red hair.

Fred fidgeted. 'I'm off, then.'

'Go, then, if you're going – and don't be too long, coming back.' Nan waved Fred away.

Ant followed him as far as the door. 'Looks a bit better, doesn't she?'

'Well done for getting her to hospital – I wish I'd been there to help.' Fred's watery blue eyes flickered over Ant with a new kind of respect.

'She put up with a lot to get here. She's brave.'

'She would, she's a fighter, see?' Fred seemed about to say something else, then he shook his head and went out.

'Bye – Grandad,' Ant called. He heard the falter in Fred's step. Then he turned back to the bed.

'You're looking well, Mrs Ball,' Kim sat down, still hand-in-hand with Mark.

'They look after me, but the food's nothing special,' Nan said. 'You're looking pleased with yourself.'

'We just got together again.'

'Be kind to each other,' said Nan. 'You might as well.'

Ant brought out a box of Malteasers to save Mark from having to make conversation. It was a standing joke between Ant and Nan who'd buy Malteasers first at Christmas. Kim brought out some grapes and Mark arranged them with the rest of her grapes.

'I'd be runnin' to the lav every five minutes, if I ate half that fruit – but thank you, anyway, dear.' She fussed with her flowered dressing gown till Ant helped her arrange it.

'Nice to hear you breathing more easily,' Mark remembered to say.

'No thanks to your cart-driving – how's Spence?'

'I've been looking after him – and Billy,' Kim chipped in. 'Likes cheese, doesn't he?'

For a while they joked about Nan's dog. Sergeant Biggins had taken Billy home after the failed search at the crossroads, and had handed him to Kim, his son's girlfriend to look after.

Ant drank in the sight of Nan in a cosy bed, flushed and chatting happily. '. . . and they say my heart's got some go in it,' she was finishing. 'I'd never've pulled through, else.'

'You're coming to stay with us,' he said, 'soon as you get out of hospital.'

'No, dear, Fred's taking care of me.'

'But he's *ancient* – I mean, he is?'

'Talking of coming out –' Kim began.

'What is it?' Nan looked from one to the other. 'Fred *told* me he got a surprise.'

'You'll have to wait,' Ant said, hugging the secret to him.

Kim and Mark grinned and got up.

'Oh, well,' Nan complained, a little testily. 'Just so everyone knows, but me.'

Everyone pictured the day Fred would call at the hospital in the smart red cart with Spence between its shafts, buffed and braided within an inch of his life and all hung about with brasses, to take her home in style. For once the engine *Kitty Hamley,* which had been the cause of their parting, would cool her wheels in her shed.

'Those poppies and butterflies up the Testing station,' Nan reminisced. 'They were a sight.' She was pinking up a little too much, now. 'And that doctor, he come up and tapped me and put me right.'

'What doctor?' asked Ant, alerted by the tapping. 'There was an officer, not a doctor.'

Then it occurred to him that Nash appeared in different guises.

'Then we had a boat-ride, didn't we? Then we were in the balloon.' She was wandering now. 'Seems like a dream to me now, and I never expected to wake up, and now you've brought me home.'

'Come on, Mark,' said Kim. 'We'll see you at home, Mrs Ball.'

'Me, too – Nan, you're tired.'

'Stay a moment, Anthony.' She caught his hand and held it.

When Mark and Kim's footsteps had died away along the corridor, Ant sat down again.

'You know I'm going somewhere soon,' Nan told him, taking his hand. 'A journey,' she repeated, firmly. 'And *you* won't be able to come with me.'

Ant felt the noise and tumult of the ward all around him, but he felt every word in his heart. *What journey?*

'You won't be able to help me, and I won't need any help. The river may be dark and broad, but I'll come to a place – a safe place – and I won't be breathless nor crippled any more, and my old bones won't ache, and nothing'll be able to hurt me, and I'll be free and light as a baby. And that evening when you see the sunset, you'll know it's true, and you'll be glad for me –'

'Nan –'

'– and you can do well at school and go on, and

one day do something you want to do, like when we looked down from the balloon – remember?'

Ant remembered the great leap up from the earth in the basket, the envelope swelling against the blue sky, the view far and wide above the teeming nuisances of the everyday world, below.

'And I'll be there somewhere – I promise.'

Ant knew then that she was right. 'And,' he managed, 'if you see a boy in an anorak up there, tell him not to bump into the clouds.'

14. First Leaf

The *Kitty Hamley* stood steaming in the Community School car park.

Fred waved from her fuel-tender. 'Anthony, want a lift home?' The tender door stood open, but a bulky plastic tank took up most of the room inside.

Ant looked up. 'What's up, Gramps?'

'Transporting used chip fat.'

'What for?'

'I'm settin' up making bio-diesel – want ter come and help me?'

Ant felt a memory uncurling in his brain. 'How d'you know how to do it?'

'I've learned the process from a chap on the moor,' his grandfather went on, climbing onto the engine. 'Outfit called Moorland Oils. Nash, he's called. Runs workshops.'

Ant stared. 'What's he like?'

'Tall chap – knows a lot. 'Course you need filtration equipment, various bits and pieces, but it's about as complicated as making good beer. I've taken a crack at it already and produced a sludge –'

'When can we start? I bet I'll be really good at it.' A picture of himself motoring from John O'Groats to Lands End on bottles of cooking oil grew in Ant's mind. It sprouted into a million possibilities.

'Oh, aye,' said Fred. 'Better'n me?'

'I want to make the best fuel ever, and set up a business selling it.' Ant felt himself growing into his future, putting out a first tentative leaf. 'You can help me set it up. Then you can go back to engines.'

'Nice of you,' said Fred.

They reached the school gates, and Ant held up his hand to stop the traffic. 'Cars everywhere,' he grumbled, 'I wish Swarf was back, sometimes.'

'Never went away,' said Fred, 'being as it's iron filings.'

'How d'you mean?'

'Swarf's a real word. Those curly bits that come off the lathe – any engineer'll tell you that. Get steering, and earn your gravy.'

Fred let off the brake and Ant spun the wheel, and *Kitty Hamley* steamed off onto the road that climbed out of the town and wound along the ridge towards the valley. 'Coming to Brewsters' fireworks, tonight?'

'The pasty giant's party? Oh, aye,' Fred said, sarcastically. He didn't think much of Brewsters. A fireworks display once a year was no replacement for workers' rights, in Fred's book.

A "thank you" Guy Fawkes night for the town, for putting up with year-long stink of pasties, a celebration for getting the world back – Ant didn't care what it was, so long as the rockets were awesome.

'Can't believe it's bonfire night, already – coming to us for Christmas?'

Fred busied himself reading the pressure gauge. 'If your mother wants me.'

Ant remembered that his mother was Fred's daughter. He remembered all the times Fred had invited him to help him in his workshop. He knew – he *must* have suspected. While steel swarf curled in shining ringlets from his metal-turning lathe, Fred must have thought about leaving his workshop to his carrot-haired grandson, some day – he should be so lucky. Ant tooted the whistle at the traffic lights.

'Coal up, Gramps.'

Fred shovelled coal into the firebox. When he straightened at last he let his hand rest on Ant's shoulder. Ant whistled proudly as they passed Brewsters, and they steamed out of town towards the moor, and school buses overtook them, and there wasn't a face pressed against the window that wouldn't have swapped places with him, for anything.

Fred didn't say much, now or ever, but now Ant had a way of knowing what his silences meant. Nan had been home, Fred had cared for her and she'd had a happy month or two. Then that journey, and that sunset, which Nan had warned Ant about, had come and gone in October, and things had worked out as she'd said, and Ant had seen that things went on, had glimpsed the secret for a moment, that worrying was human and pointless.

And he'd started Year Nine, and it had been all right, and he'd learned riding from Kim and gone out on Spence a few times, and Midgeley the cat had waxed fat – Ant liked that phrase – on the new cat biscuits he was trying him on, and a notice had been put up on The Point reminding people how dangerous it was. And now he was going to learn removing water from used chip-fat, and heating it up with lye to make diesel. He and his gramps weren't the only ones making less damaging fuel – the world was busy turning in a new direction, like a daisy following the sun, and he, Ant, would be a part of it. But first he'd visit Nan.

Ant let the lovely evening light lead him along the lane. He gathered grasses and spiky things he didn't know the name of, as he neared the little cemetery – he thought she'd like them better than carnations bought at Sharpe's.

He entered by the rusty gate, and the valley lay breathless beneath him. Between purple hills in the far distance, the river gleamed away to the sea.

'Katherine Grace Ball', read the simple granite tombstone. 'Laid To Rest October 15th.'

Ant pictured Nan kicking up her heels at the family Christmas party. She had too much life to Rest. He laid his hedgerow flowers on her grave and tidied her gravel a little. For a moment, he wished he had her umbrella handle to remember her by. He remembered giving it to Alice. Then he realised he'd never need anything to remember Nan by, ever, for as long as he lived, because she was unforgettable. He reburied a crocus bulb under a corner of her turf, and then he found Nature Boy.

'Stuart James Diamond', the gravestone read, simply. 'Fourteen Years And Six Months.' The memorial didn't feel as if it had anything to do with the boy who'd haunted the hill, who had cared so much about its animals. Ant closed the gate and turned up the road to the quarry. When he felt the wind bluster around him on the highest point of the rocks, saw the fluted granite walls and the lake beneath them like a marble floor under organ pipes, he knew he was in the right place to remember Stu.

Ant surveyed the view to the horizon. The busy world moved on, below. Still everyone remembered the fuel lockup in some small part of their brain, used petrol a little more thoughtfully, and the flowers at Heartsease Cross wagged in the exhaust of a few less cars, every day.

Buses called more often along the main road and people used them more, and sometimes birds could be heard around the village as clearly as on the Days After The Dust. There was even a plan to mark the anniversary of the first day of the green jelly as Swarving Day, when everyone would leave their cars at home to hear again, that silence.

Ant wasn't sure it would stick.

But now and again he'd climb the ridge to sit at the lip of Stu's Point, and whenever he looked out over the great, silent bowl of the landscape, a feeling of fullness filled his heart. And if, after a while, he spotted Markie or Kim or Mum or Dad climbing up to join him, and if they'd brought with them a pasty or two, well, that made it so much better.